EYES

OF THE

FOREST

W9-DFP-447

0 0022 0629317 3

AR CASS COUNTY PUBLIC LIBRARY
400 E. MECHANIC
HARRISONVILLE, MO 64701

HONORS FOR APRIL HENRY

Edgar Award Finalist

Anthony Award Winner

ALA Best Books for Young Adults

ALA Quick Picks for Young Adults

Barnes & Noble Top Teen Pick

Winner of the Maryland Black-Eyed Susan Book Award

Missouri Truman Readers Award Selection

TLA Tayshas Selection

New York State Charlotte Award Winner

Oregon Spirit Award Winner

One Book for Nebraska Teens

Nebraska Golden Sower Honor Book

YALSA Quick Pick for Reluctant YA Readers

EYES

OF THE

FOREST

OTHER MYSTERIES BY APRIL HENRY

Girl, Stolen

The Night She Disappeared

The Girl Who Was Supposed to Die

The Girl I Used to Be

Count All Her Bones

The Lonely Dead

Run, Hide, Fight Back

The Girl in the White Van

Playing with Fire

THE POINT LAST SEEN SERIES:

The Body in the Woods

Blood Will Tell

PRAISE FOR

EYES OF THE FOREST

"*Eyes of the Forest* by April Henry (*The Lonely Dead*) is a suspenseful, captivating look at what may happen when a fantasy world becomes too real for some of its fans ... Henry's engaging and often thrilling narrative is told from multiple points of view, allowing readers close access to the motivations of all her main characters. She expertly examines the darker side of the culture of fandom, including pressures it puts on creators, and how fans themselves get out of hand."

—Shelf Awareness

"When the police do not believe that Portland, Oregon, author R. M. Haldon has been kidnapped, it's up to his young researcher, Bridget Shepherd, to save him ... Excellent pacing, shifting between the perspectives of the main characters, adds to the suspenseful feeling of a ticking clock, and readers come to understand everyone's motivations ... Offers a suspenseful and dastardly plot entwined with fan culture and mystery."

—Kirkus Reviews

"In this mystery with a clever twist by Henry (*Playing with Fire*), a George R. R. Martin–esque author is forced to write in captivity, his only hope of rescue lying with his teenage Portland, Ore.–based assistant ... Its brisk pacing and sensational premise will have wide appeal."

—Publishers Weekly

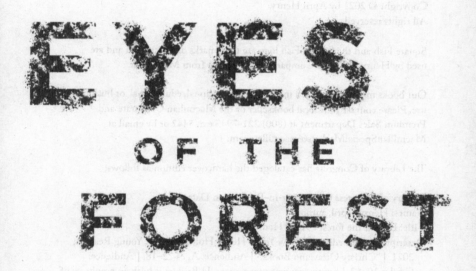

EYES
OF THE
FOREST

APRIL HENRY

SQUARE
FISH

Christy Ottaviano Books

HENRY HOLT AND COMPANY

NEW YORK

SQUARE
FISH

An imprint of Macmillan Publishing Group, LLC
120 Broadway, New York, NY 10271 • fiercereads.com

Copyright © 2021 by April Henry.
All rights reserved.

Square Fish and the Square Fish logo are trademarks of Macmillan and are
used by Henry Holt and Company under license from Macmillan.

Our books may be purchased in bulk for promotional, educational, or business
use. Please contact your local bookseller or the Macmillan Corporate and
Premium Sales Department at (800) 221-7945 ext. 5442 or by email at
MacmillanSpecialMarkets@macmillan.com.

The Library of Congress has cataloged the hardcover edition as follows:

Library of Congress Cataloging-in-Publication Data
Names: Henry, April, author.
Title: Eyes of the forest / April Henry.
Description: First edition. | New York : Henry Holt Books for Young Readers,
    2021. | "Christy Ottaviano Books." | Audience: Ages 12–18. | Audience:
    Grades 10–12. | Summary: Seventeen-year-old Bridget is both an employee of
    author R. M. Haldon and his biggest fan, so when she starts to receive cryptic
    emails from him after he goes missing, she teams up with her friend to find
    Haldon.
Identifiers: LCCN 2020038061 | ISBN 9781250234087 (hardcover)
Subjects: CYAC: Missing persons—Fiction. | Fans (Persons)—Fiction. |
    Authors—Fiction. | Authorship—Fiction. | Books and reading—Fiction.
Classification: LCC PZ7.H39356 Ey 2021 | DDC [Fic]—dc23
LC record available at https://lccn.loc.gov/2020038061

Originally published in the United States by Henry Holt and Company
First Square Fish edition, 2022
Book designed by Mike Burroughs and Mallory Grigg
Image on frontispiece, half-title page, and chapter openers used under license
from Shutterstock.
Square Fish logo designed by Filomena Tuosto
Printed in the United States of America

ISBN 978-1-250-83324-2 (paperback)
10 9 8 7 6 5 4 3

AR: 5.3 / LEXILE: HL750L

To Robert C. O'Brien,
Samuel Shellabarger, Stephen King,
Susan Fromberg Schaeffer,
Lee Smith, Marge Piercy,
George R. R. Martin,
and all the other writers
who have held me enthralled.

R. M. HALDON RELIES ON TEENAGE RESEARCHER AS HE WRITES *EYES OF THE FOREST*

Have you ever loved a story so much that you dreamed of becoming part of it?

For Bridget S. (she asked us not to use her full last name), what for most people is just a dream has become her reality. The now-seventeen-year-old was only twelve when she met R. M. Haldon at a signing, where she impressed him with her encyclopedic knowledge of his series. Haldon hired her to create a database containing Swords and Shadows' myriad details.

When Haldon recently mentioned Bridget at a fan convention, ardent aficionados wanted to know more about her work with the master.

We reached out to Bridget by email to talk about her collaboration with Haldon, how she keeps track of all those details, and why she thinks the books are better than the TV series.

What's it like to work with R. M. Haldon?

It's pretty much all done by email. He sends me questions, like asking if he's mentioned any heraldry with nine-pointed stars, or what he's written about a particular king. Sometimes I ask him questions, too. Like when one character's death was not depicted on the page, I asked if he was really dead.

And what was his answer?
I'm afraid my lips are sealed.

How do you keep track of all the details?
I approach it one page at a time, sorting out where everything belongs.

How many times have you read the books?
To be honest, I've lost count.

Is it hard juggling your work for Haldon as well as schoolwork?
I'm a good student, and I've kept up my grades. That's one of the agreements I made with my dad before he let me do this. I have to maintain a 3.5 average. I've never gotten below 3.8.

What do you think of the TV show?
The TV show's good, of course, at times even great. But because of the limitations of TV, they've had to compress storylines or even cut entire subplots. And for me, it's the details that make the books so good.

When do you think we'll finally see _Eyes of the Forest_?
He's doing the best he can, but it's a huge task. I'm sure when we finally see it, it will be amazing.

I don't understand fans who have turned against him because the last book will publish later than originally planned. Even if there's never an end to the series, I don't care. It will never take away those hours of pleasure the books provided for all of us. I'm just thankful he's given us what he has.

BOB

The Gun

The gun looked real. No orange tip, no obvious seams where molded plastic pieces had been glued together.

Although who was Bob kidding? He could tell a dirk from a stiletto, but modern weapons were a mystery.

Besides, the important thing about this gun was that it was pointed at his chest. The end of the barrel was just a few inches from his heart. Adrenaline jolted through him.

"Get in the trunk," the young man ordered.

Bob raised his hands in a placating gesture. "Please, Derrick. I just—"

"Shut up," Derrick barked. "I don't want to hear another word out of you, understand?"

"But—"

The word hadn't even left Bob's mouth before the butt of the gun connected with his temple.

Bob's last, half-formed thought was that the gun certainly *felt* real.

BRIDGET

Compelled to Change by an Outside Force

Queen Jeyne regarded the assassin," a voice murmured
in Bridget's left ear. "'You must find the babe, and you
must kill it. Or you and your family will die screaming.'"

Belatedly, Bridget realized Mr. Manning was eyeing
her. She straightened up and looked at him attentively. She
resisted the urge to check if her hair completely covered
the single earbud and the short stretch of wire that disappeared under the collar of her shirt. Normally it wasn't hard
to listen to an audiobook and a teacher simultaneously, but
physics was sometimes challenging.

"While it's true that a falling apple got Isaac Newton
thinking about gravity," Mr. Manning said, "there's no
evidence one hit him on the head. But he did start wondering why apples always fall down, rather than sideways
or even up."

He still seemed focused on Bridget, so she tried to
look intent as he explained how Newton had postulated
that everything in the universe was attracted to everything else in the universe. Calculating the degree of
attraction required a complicated formula, but it basically

depended on how far apart the two objects were, as well as their mass.

Walker's stage whisper came from the last row, perfectly pitched to reach the other students but not Mr. Manning. "If that's true, then how come I'm not attracted to fat girls?"

As the offensive comment earned him a few snorts, Bridget exchanged an eye roll with Ajay, one row over.

Sensing trouble, Mr. Manning began to roam the aisles as he talked about mass and universal gravitation. Bridget's attention soon returned to the fine thread of sound connecting her to another, far more interesting, world.

The audiobook's narrator had moved on to the hunt for the baby. In her mind's eye, Bridget was beside the assassin as he snuck down an alley. Together they looked up, trying to spot foot- and handholds in the rough wall. Once he climbed into the attic room, the assassin planned to kill Jancy, the newborn baby now lying in the arms of her mother, a serving girl named Margarit. It was Margarit's misfortune that one night, nine months ago, she'd caught the king's eye. And that a seer had prophesied one of the king's children would grow up to overthrow him.

The only solution seemed to be to order the murder of his own offspring, but the king had balked. When it came to his illegitimate children, Queen Jeyne was not nearly as squeamish.

"Newton began developing the laws of motion when he was only twenty-three. Just six years older than you guys," Mr. Manning said. "Derrick, can you tell me the first law of motion?" He liked to randomly call on students.

Derrick, a tall, skinny guy with a bad complexion, straightened up. Bridget had never talked to him, but she knew who he was. Everyone at school did—for all the wrong reasons.

"Basically, it says a body at rest will remain at rest, and a body in motion will remain in motion, unless they are compelled to change by an outside force."

Walker made a sotto voce comment about bodies in motion, but Bridget paid no attention. The book was approaching one of her favorite scenes. The voice in her ear painted a picture of a cramped room, barely big enough to hold a straw-stuffed mattress. The low ceiling forced the assassin to stoop as he crept forward. The image was so vivid that Bridget reflexively hunched her shoulders. On the bed a sleeping Margarit lay curled around her baby. She was a long-legged, milk-white girl of some six-and-ten years. A healthy wench, to look at her. At least, the narrator warned, she would be until the assassin's dagger entered her heart.

A dagger. Was this dagger in the database? Bridget jotted in the notebook hidden under her classroom notes. R. M. Haldon's fantasies were famous for the wide variety of weapons the characters wielded, from dirks to double-bladed axes to the misericorde, a long narrow knife used to deliver a merciful death to gravely wounded knights.

Even though she was focused on the details, the overall story still enthralled Bridget. It didn't matter that she'd heard or read it more than a dozen times before. That she knew how the assassin's mission would fail, or how the blind seer's prophecy would come true in surprising ways.

Bridget was so enraptured that she didn't notice Mr. Manning had stopped speaking. Didn't glimpse him creeping up behind her. Didn't hear Ajay's frantic throat clearing.

And then the teacher's fingers plucked away her earbud. She let out a shocked bleat as he held it out of reach, the wire stretched tight.

"Hand me your phone," Mr. Manning ordered.

She slipped her phone from her pocket. In order to give it to him, she had to pop the earbud wire from the jack. When she did, the narrator's plummy tones suddenly filled the classroom.

His dagger was poised to plunge into the sleeping girl, when to his surprise, he saw a knife glinting in her left hand. The blade was as thin as she was. Then the point was under his chin, pressing his head up.

"Drop it," Margarit said calmly. When he did not comply, she twisted her own blade. The babe whimpered as a trickle of blood, looking more black than red, dripped onto its skin. She whispered, "Sleep, Jancy."

The assassin—

Mr. Manning stabbed a button on her phone, and it mercifully fell silent. "Was that *King of Swords*?" he asked, incredulous. It was clear he'd expected to hear a popular song, not a book published before Bridget was born.

Its age didn't stop anyone from enjoying it now. Haldon lived in a Portland suburb, but people all over the world had read *King of Swords*, its sequels, or the graphic novel adaption, or at least seen the spin-off TV show.

Bridget nodded. Her cheeks were on fire. She cursed her redhead's complexion for betraying her. She'd been caught on her phone before, but at least then no one had known exactly what she was listening to. Were people now going to lump her in with Derrick, known school-wide as the weird loner who spent his weekends live-action role-playing—LARPing—in a game inspired by Swords and Shadows? Because while it was mostly fine to be a fan, there was an unspoken line, and once you were perceived to have crossed it, you became a socially inept, geeky pariah.

Behind her, Walker was saying something about "queen of kooks," but Bridget ignored him.

She sat in miserable silence until class ended and Mr. Manning handed her phone back. As she gathered her things, Ajay leaned over.

"All that trouble just for a book?" He raised one eyebrow, but his dark eyes were friendly. Whenever Mr. Manning or Walker was being unbelievably annoying, they would trade glances and the occasional whisper.

"It's not just *a* book." She lowered her voice as Derrick walked by. She was relieved that he wasn't seeking her out. "It's *King of Swords* by R. M. Haldon."

"Those books always look so thick." With his fingers, Ajay measured a space about four inches high. "And I'm not a big reader."

"You haven't even seen the TV show?"

He shrugged.

"You have no idea what you're missing."

"Want to fill me in over lunch?"

For a moment, Bridget forgot about the assassin, Margarit, and Jancy. She forgot to think at all. There was only Ajay, standing close enough she was aware of the warmth emanating from his skin and the faint smell of ginger on his clothes. Ajay, with his thick black brows and friendly dark eyes. Ajay, who had been whispering little asides to her all fall. Ajay, who was now shifting from foot to foot, waiting for her answer.

If she were a character, what would she do? Simper? Flirt? Turn down Ajay and leave him disconsolate? More than nearly anyone in the world, Bridget could imagine how she might handle this situation if it were fictional.

But it wasn't. And she wasn't a queen or a peasant girl or a courtesan. She was just Bridget. And all she could think of to say was a faint, "Sure."

BOB

How Far Would He Make It?

Bob's eyes fluttered open. Someone had shouted. It might have been him.

His head hurt. With effort, he traced the memory back. Derrick had *hurt* him. *Derrick.*

Was his skull broken? With a groan, Bob pushed himself up on one elbow. He was in a bed in a room he didn't recognize. He stared in horror at the stains obscuring the pillowcase's tiny faded blue flowers. Blood. *His* blood.

Gritting his teeth, he touched his scalp. The wound was about an inch long, just above his temple. He pressed his fingers on his crew cut, tacky with blood. The skin had been split, but the skull underneath seemed intact.

A surge of relief rolled over him, followed immediately by a pulse of anxiety. What if he'd just exposed the wound to new germs? What if that half-formed scab was the only thing protecting him from a nasty infection right next to his brain? Back in the Middle Ages, you might not die from the battlefield wound, but from the infection that followed.

His stomach roiled as he thought of something else. He'd shouted as he woke. What if Derrick came back and hurt him again?

Bob strained his ears, but heard nothing. After pushing himself to a sitting position, he looked around. He was in a small bedroom, about twelve by fourteen feet. The walls were yellow pine, dotted with brown knotholes. The door was closed. The fir floor was bare.

Bob still couldn't believe what had happened. Derrick snarling at him to get in the trunk. The *Is that real?* gun that now seemed likely to be. The sickening crunch against his skull as he felt his bones turn to jelly. The engulfing darkness.

Bob was trembling, and it wasn't just from the chilly air. Things were horribly wrong.

When he swung his legs over the edge of the bed, there was a metallic clatter. Clamped around his ankles, over his socks, was what looked like a pair of handcuffs connected with a chain. A six-foot-long plastic-coated cable had been threaded through the cuff around his right ankle. The other end was looped around the leg of a desk a few feet away. The desk, made of aluminum and plastic, looked incongruously modern in the otherwise rustic setting. Under the desk was a built-in treadmill.

Bob was still wearing the same clothes in which he'd been taken. The same clothes he always wore. A plain black T-shirt and blue jeans. But what about his scarf? A second of panic before his fingers found it, still around his neck. No coat. His old white Nikes were nowhere in sight. Without the blanket's warmth, the cold was already sinking into his marrow.

In front of the treadmill desk, the single window was framed by white curtains. Outside, an expanse of white snow and massive evergreens.

Derrick had told Bob about this cabin, tucked away in the forest. No landline. No Wi-Fi. Just electricity and running water—if a storm didn't take them out.

Even if Bob managed to free himself, how far would he make it without shoes? He had researched frostbite, and it wasn't pretty. While he wasn't a big walker, without toes it would be even harder.

Between the bed and the treadmill desk was a nightstand overflowing with provisions. A brown Pyrex bowl filled with apples, bananas, oranges, pears. A bag of baby carrots. Six plastic water bottles. A loaf of Dave's Killer Bread. A brick of Tillamook cheddar. But no knife to cut it with. No utensils at all.

Nothing Bob could use to free himself. To attack someone. Or hurt himself.

The treadmill desk held, somewhat incongruously, a typewriter. A black Royal. Sitting next to it was a neat stack of blank white paper. The rest of the desktop was bare.

A single sheet of paper had been folded in half and propped on top of the typewriter. On it was scrawled,

Better start writing Eyes of the Forest. Or else!

Bob took stock. He was in an isolated cabin, injured, shackled. No one but his captors knew where he was.

Maybe hurting him had surprised Derrick as much as it had Bob. Or wouldn't he have put out painkillers, antiseptic, and bandages to go with the food? Other than the furniture, the room was bare. No TV, no magazines, no books. Not even any framed posters.

Nothing to distract him.

Bob shifted uncomfortably. Pressure, low in his belly. He had to pee. Presumably there was a bathroom someplace. He mentally measured the distance to the door and then the cable. It didn't seem good.

He got to his feet, briefly closing his eyes against a wave of dizziness. The cable pulled him up short before he reached the door. Bob leaned forward. The tips of his fingers just closed around the knob.

He pulled it open, revealing a narrow hallway and letting in air that was, if anything, even colder. From this vantage point, he couldn't see other rooms. It didn't matter anyway, because Bob couldn't reach them. Even if he managed to drag the treadmill behind him, it wouldn't fit through the doorway.

The pressure in his bladder was worse. "Derrick!" he yelled. "Derrick!"

No answer. The cabin was silent.

He was turning back when he spotted it. Squatting under the bed was a white ceramic pot the size of a mixing bowl. If it had been one-fifth the size, it might have been mistaken for serving ware. Perhaps a specialized vessel for cream or gravy that would appear only on Grandma's table at Thanksgiving.

But Bob knew exactly what it was. What it was for. A jordan, a jerry, a guzunder, a po, a chamber utensil, a thunder pot. A potty. A well-used item for centuries, across cultures, across continents, at least until the flush toilet had been invented.

"Oh, hell no," Bob said.

BRIDGET

Never Take Anything for Granted

Ajay followed Bridget down the hall to the cafeteria. "So why were you listening to that book in class?" With each step, the smell of old grease intensified.

"Because I love it." She grabbed a black plastic tray, then held up two fingers for the cafeteria lady. "Two tacos, please. With cheese." She turned back to Ajay. "Aren't you getting anything?"

"I bring my own lunch."

"Oh." In high school, that was true of hardly anyone. She associated bringing your lunch with people whose parents were too proud to take free lunch. Or people who were allergic to gluten or dairy or peanut butter. Or whose moms drew hearts on the outside of the paper bag and slipped a Post-it inside that said *Have a great day*.

The way her own mom used to.

"I've seen you listening to your phone in other classes." Ajay followed her to the big metal bowl of fruit. "I always thought it was music, but now I'm guessing it must have been a book. So what makes it worth getting your phone taken away?"

Inspecting an apple, Bridget tried to articulate her

feelings. "All the books in the Swords and Shadows series are amazing. They're filled with bravery, treachery, and sacrifice." She gestured at the fluorescent lights, the chipped linoleum floor, the hordes of students. "This is the boring real world, where Portland, Oregon, and Portland, Maine, are pretty much interchangeable. But in those books, there aren't any high schools or Walmarts or Taco Tuesdays."

"Hey, a lot of people like Taco Tuesdays," Ajay objected, following Bridget to the cashier.

"And in those books, you can never take anything for granted." She handed the cashier her cafeteria card. "You know how if you watch a movie, there's always certain characters you don't really have to worry about?"

"Like the cute five-year-old who keeps saying surprisingly wise things?" Ajay offered. "But no matter how bad things get, that kid always survives the vampires or the earthquake or the serial killer or whatever."

"Exactly." Bridget picked up her tray. "In the Swords and Shadows series, a five-year-old could and maybe would die. And the reader might even have to watch." She hesitated. Normally she sat on the edge of the cafeteria with a book and Ajay sat in the middle with friends.

"Want to eat outside?" he said. Now that the temperature was dropping, only a few people were sitting at the concrete benches and tables.

"Um, sure."

As they walked past his regular table, a couple of his friends nudged each other. He didn't seem to notice. In the far corner, Derrick was peering intently at his phone.

Outside, they found an empty table. Next to them, a couple was enthusiastically kissing. On the other side, a boy exhaled his vape smoke into his hoodie.

Ajay unzipped his backpack. "Okay, give me the basic rundown of the plot."

"For the whole series? That's like explaining how the entire world works to an alien who just landed here." But if anyone was up to the task, Bridget figured she was. "Do the best you can."

AJAY

Struck a Nerve

Ajay still couldn't believe he was doing this. Asking a girl to have lunch with him. And judging from the expressions of his friends staring at him through the cafeteria window, they couldn't believe it either. Feeling self-conscious, he looked down as he pulled a large, shiny cloth bag from his backpack.

"Wait, what's that made out of?" Reaching out, Bridget grazed the stiff cloth with her fingers.

"Waxed cotton. Like, literally beeswax. To fold it, you warm it up with your hands." Her expression seemed oddly unhappy. "What's the matter? Usually people think it's cool. This new company in Beaverton is making them."

Two spots of color appeared in her cheeks. "Don't hate me, but my dad sells food-grade plastic for this company called Triple P. Mostly plastic wrap."

Plastic? That went against everything Ajay stood for. But then again, it was Bridget's dad. Not Bridget.

"No offense, but I just don't like things that are going to live on for centuries after I use them once." From the bag, Ajay took out metal utensils, a cloth napkin, and a tiffin.

Bridget looked intrigued by the series of interlocking stainless steel containers. "What's that?"

"A tiffin box. It's like the Indian equivalent of a lunch box." Ajay began unsnapping the clasps that held the flat round containers together.

"It's clever. All those separate layers. What's in each of them?"

Ajay pointed at the bottom one. "Rice." His finger moved to the middle. "That's kachumber salad—diced cucumber, tomato, and red onion, with cilantro and lemon-cumin dressing."

"Yum." She peered closer.

"And the top one is called moong dal. It's made with mung beans and garlic cooked in butter and spices." As he spoke, he spooned it over the rice.

Bridget inhaled appreciatively. "It smells wonderful. Your mom must be a great cook."

"My mom?" Ajay chuckled. "Sexist much?" Sure, in his grandparents' generation, the women did all the cooking, even down to reheating foods in the microwave, but times had changed.

"Oh, sorry." Her face reddened again. "Your dad."

Ajay was enjoying himself. "Excuse me, but I am the one who made everything."

"Wait—what?"

"I've been the main cook at my house since seventh grade." His mom was a pediatrician with a busy practice, and, frankly, not much of a cook. He'd learned to cook in self-defense. He filled the spoon with rice and beans. "Want a bite?"

"Um, sure." At first she chewed quickly, as if she wanted to get it over with. Then she slowed down.

"That's more than just cooking," she said. "That's like magic. At our house, we mostly heat up food from Trader Joe's. Sometimes if I'm feeling adventurous, I'll combine bags of various frozen things."

Ajay kept his face neutral, although inwardly he flinched. Before he took over the cooking duties, his mom's approach to making roti had been to buy it at Trader Joe's and nuke it in the microwave. Trader Joe's food wasn't bad, but it certainly wasn't home-cooked.

Ajay reminded himself that he hadn't come out here to talk about himself, but to listen to Bridget. "You still need to explain those books to me."

"Okay, in the first book, *King of Swords*, there's this baby, Jancy. She's the illegitimate daughter of the king and a serving wench. But after a seer prophesied that one of the king's children would grow up to overthrow him, the queen ordered all his illegitimate children killed." Bridget took a bite of her taco.

"Harsh," Ajay mumbled as he chewed. "Are there a lot of kids?"

"At least a dozen, and he keeps making more. When you're a king, you can get away with a lot of bad behavior." Bridget shrugged. "But Jancy's mother managed to save her from the assassin. Then to keep her safe, she gave her to the Skin Changers to raise."

"What are Skin Changers?"

"They can look like anything: a person, an animal, even a tree. But to be one, you need to be capable of that kind of magic, and Jancy isn't. The Skin Changers do teach her how to fight with swords and daggers and just her bare hands. And it's been pretty clear for the last couple of books that Jancy does have a magical talent. But so far it hasn't been revealed."

"Okay." Ajay was more or less following.

"And at the end of the last book, the king died, just like in the prophecy. But it wasn't clear if Jancy caused his death, although she was blamed for it. The prophecy, like all prophecies, is subject to interpretation. And parts still haven't been fulfilled. Readers really want to know what's going to happen next."

Ajay nodded. "Even I know that that Haldon guy is late turning in the last one in the series. Is that why you're listening to that old book—because there aren't any new ones?"

Her blue eyes sparked. "I don't ever get tired of it. There's always some new detail. And it's not really his fault it's late. *Eyes of the Forest* is going to be the last in the series. Bob's going to have to tie everything up and answer all the questions he's raised in the other books. Who's going to win control of the kingdom and the magical mirror? Will the winged unicorns choose to fight with humans in the final battle against the Armies of the Night? Will Prince Orwen really help Jancy fight the undead, or will he betray her and join the Dark Emperor? And is he even really King Tristan's son?" Bridget's words sped up. "And who is Jancy's true love—Prince Orwen or Rowan, the leader of the peasant rebellion?"

Ajay tried to hold on to the pieces he had followed.

"If their father is the same guy, isn't Prince Orwen really Jancy's half brother?" Before she could answer, he moved on. "Orwen and Rowan? Orwen and Rowan?" The two names were nearly identical. "How can you keep them straight?"

She looked defensive. Ajay realized, too late, that he had struck a nerve. "You try naming literally thousands of characters. It's not easy."

Something she'd said had been nagging him. "Wait a minute. Go back. You said some guy named Bob had to tie up everything with this last book. Aren't they written by R. M. Haldon?"

Now the color spread from her cheeks to the rest of her face. "R. M. stands for Robert Mark. But he goes by Bob."

"You almost sound like you know him. Doesn't he live somewhere around here?" Ajay had seen Haldon in magazines and on TV. He was your standard middle-aged white guy, except that he always wore a violet silk scarf around his neck.

Bridget looked away. "Those books have been part of my life for a long time. I started reading them when I was eight."

"Eight?" He was shocked, remembering the single episode of the TV show he had seen. It had seemed too graphic, even for him. "Isn't that way too young?"

"I snuck the first one from my mom. She was a big fan."

"Was?" Ajay echoed. "She doesn't like them anymore?"

Bridget swallowed. "She's dead."

BOB

I Don't Think You Understand

The need to pee had finally trumped Bob's vow not to use the chamber pot. Afterward he'd shoved it back under the bed and tried to forget about it. Instead, he focused on the note.

Better start writing Eyes of the Forest. Or else!

From a writerly standpoint, Bob appreciated Derrick leaving the "or else" for him to fill in. The unknown was far worse than the known. And the reader always conjured up a more frightening threat than the writer could.

Derrick wasn't the only one who wanted Bob to finish *Eyes of the Forest*. Everyone was mad at him, starting with his publisher.

The last time he'd seen Jamie, his editor, had been a few months ago. Bob had been in New York for a fantasy con, and Jamie insisted on taking him out to dinner. It was the kind of restaurant with no menus.

Soon after they were seated, the waiter set down a mirrored tray. On it a short candle flickered next to a crusty loaf and lines of spices.

No plates. They must be meant to share. At medieval banquets, the lord's plate was piled high. If he so desired, everyone at the table could share his food, a high honor indeed.

Bob wondered which one of them was the lord in this scenario.

He sniffed. The candle smelled delicious—and oddly familiar.

The waiter pointed. "Semolina baguette, accompanied by sumac, Maldon sea salt, spicebush berries, and our edible beef tallow candle. The chef made it by infusing rendered beef fat with rosemary, sage, and thyme."

As he spoke, he snuck a glance at Bob. It was getting harder and harder to be anonymous. At least at this restaurant there were fewer chances a stranger would demand a selfie or beg to be cast in the TV show.

Jamie leaned forward and gently blew out the flame.

Mouth watering, Bob tore off a section of bread. "Spreading animal fat on bread is an old practice," he noted, smearing the hunk over what had been a candle. "Beef tallow was used in eighteenth-century England to moisten stale loaves."

Jamie smiled his tight little smile. "That's one reason I thought you'd love this place. They bring the same passion to food you do to your books." He smoothed his napkin over his thighs. His lapis blue suit was snug, not because he'd gained weight, but because that seemed to have become the fashion. His pants were as close as a second skin. It must be uncomfortable to sit. His shoes were the color of mahogany, with silver buckles, shiny and impregnable. Bob tucked his battered Nikes out of sight.

In the Swords and Shadows series, the clothing of the wealthy was richly detailed with embroidery and trimmed with fur. Their arms, ears, fingers, and necks were festooned with gold jewelry studded with precious gems.

Serena, the TV show's wardrobe mistress, constantly pressed Bob for details. Would the petticoat under the queen's dress be made of silk or cotton or linen? "A lot of TVs are the size of a movie screen now," she'd told him. "After three or four viewings, fans start to notice even the tiniest details. That's why we go to all this effort."

The last time Bob had been on set, she'd shown off the costumes for the fisherfolk. "We wove the fabric out of heavy wool and then coated it with fish oil to make it waterproof." When Serena held one out to him, Bob was forced to step back, his hand over his nose. The smell was a dumpster on a hot day. "They do stink," she said, "but they're authentic."

Authentic to what? Bob had asked himself. To what he'd imagined sitting alone in his suburban study, cramming Doritos into his mouth and then typing on his plastic keyboard with orange-coated fingers?

Nearly a hundred people worked under Serena, and she had more specialists on call. Bob's words employed weavers, embroiderers, leather workers, armorers, and jewelers. To make the costumes appear realistically worn, a halfdozen textile artists were responsible for destroying and then repairing them.

While Serena implied she would source the actual

hides of flying unicorns if she could, an underling had once admitted to Bob that the rough black fur capes worn by the Armies of the Night had started life as IKEA area rugs with holes cut in the center for heads.

Now Jamie looked at Bob meaningfully. He hadn't taken a single bite. "So you've probably guessed what I want to talk about."

Bob didn't answer. No good could come from talking about the book, which was years overdue. He tore off another hunk of bread, smeared it in the fat and spices, and stuffed it in his mouth.

"I know this is delicate, Bob, but how is *Eyes of the Forest* coming along? I would love to schedule it. Of course it will be our lead title. We'll build everything else around it for the season. For the year."

Bob pointed at his mouth, making a show of chewing. The true answer was the book was barely begun, but that clearly wasn't a *good* answer.

The waiter whisked away the remains of the bread. Seconds later, he was back with two scallop shells. "Scallop crudo served alongside its roe, smoked both on wood and over wood."

Bob didn't know what most of that meant, except he was pretty sure crudo meant raw. He picked up the fork the waiter had brought and slowly put a piece in his mouth. It was rubbery. The roe popped between his teeth.

Bob forced himself to swallow. While his characters ate pies with real animal claws poking out of the crust, or roasted peacocks re-dressed in their own feathers, he himself was not an adventurous eater.

He still hadn't answered Jamie.

The other man broke the silence. "We need this book, Bob. I don't think you understand how much. The last time the house was solidly in the black was the year *Mountains of the Moon* published."

That was well over three years ago. The publisher had kept the book in hardcover for more than two years, milking every last drop of profit, before finally releasing a trade paper edition. At one point, both the paperback *and* the hardcover had been on the bestseller lists. They had also issued a collector's edition bound in lambskin, and floated the idea of an "even more unique" edition printed with ink mixed with some of Bob's blood ("Just one tube, Bob.").

He'd rejected the idea. But tonight he'd come prepared to say yes if it would get Jamie off his back.

After taking away the shells, the waiter returned with two plates. "House-made pasta with local mushrooms collected by our on-staff forager, topped with an egg cooked in a spoon."

An on-staff forager? An egg cooked in a spoon? Bob shot Jamie an amused glance, but it was not returned. His editor would not be deterred.

The books weren't just Bob alone in a room with his thoughts anymore. Now hundreds of people depended on him. Thousands. Not just for entertainment, but for work. His agent, his publisher, all the foreign publishers, the bookstores. The TV show was just finishing up filming *Mountains of the Moon*, which they had broken into two seasons. But after that, there was no more source material. Then all those people—from the showrunner to Serena and on down to the stuntmen and caterers—would be out of a job.

It was too much pressure. Bob had never asked for it. He just wanted to tell stories that interested him. Stories that surprised him. Where the characters refused to do what he'd planned and instead did something so unexpected all he could do was move his fingers over the keys and describe what he saw with his mind's eye.

Jamie filled the silence. "I'm guessing that after more than twenty years, you don't want the series to end, Bob, but it doesn't have to." He leaned forward, not noticing as his tie pressed against a tallow smear on the tablecloth the waiter had missed. "No one is going to complain if what was originally supposed to be your last book isn't. Just give us a book. Any book. We can copyedit and get it out within eight weeks, like we did last time."

"I'm working on it," Bob said. "It's going to be big, and big takes time."

"Then give us the first half. We'll put it out in two volumes."

He made a face. "Just because they did that with the TV show doesn't mean I can. That's not how books work for me."

They paused for the waiter to serve "hay-smoked beef and polenta parchment." If Bob's mouth was full, it gave him an excuse not to talk. So he kept doggedly eating as one plate replaced another. Gnocchi and cuttlefish and squab and lamb and finally dessert. The servings were small, and they ate with forks (a fifteenth-century invention that had originally been considered blasphemous, a rejection of God-made fingers), but the elaborate meal wouldn't have been out of place at a king's court. All it lacked was jugglers, a court fool, and staged pageantry between courses.

Finally, Bob leaned back with a groan. "Jamie, can I ask you a serious question?"

"Of course."

"Are you trying to kill me? Are you thinking if I drop dead of a heart attack you could hire a ghostwriter?"

Jamie looked shocked, but was it an act? They must have considered what would happen if he died before finishing the series.

Once you started typing in the Google search bar, it would helpfully autocomplete the most-searched-for phrases. So Bob knew what words came to mind when people thought of him:

rm haldon weight
rm haldon sick
rm haldon heart attack
rm haldon age
rm haldon diabetes
rm haldon health
is rm haldon dying
is rm haldon writing

On Reddit and Goodreads and Amazon, fans posted they were worried about him. Opined that he wasn't looking so great. That he was overweight. That he was sixty-one. That the way he was going, he might not be around to finish the series.

And, according to his fans, he owed them. They were angry he played video games. Resentful he watched basketball. Upset he went to movies. They didn't want him to travel for conventions or research.

He'd even gotten hate mail saying he should be shackled to a typewriter until he finished the book.

Now Bob looked at the cable connecting him to the desk. It seemed they had gotten their wish.

BRIDGET

Something in Common

O h." Ajay's eyes were big. "I'm sorry about your mom." Two years ago, he'd moved to Portland from Seattle, so he only knew the Bridget she was now, not the Bridget she'd been as a kid. The Bridget who used to laugh a lot. The Bridget who'd had friends, until she had pared them all away to focus on her dying mother.

She took a deep breath. "I shouldn't have said it so abruptly. My mom had cancer, so it wasn't like her death came as a surprise. There were three or four years where she was either undergoing treatment or trying to recover. No matter what the doctors did, the cancer always came back. But those books—they took her out of herself. I begged her to read them to me, but she said I was too young. So I snuck *King of Swords* into my room and read it when my parents were asleep." As she spoke, she felt her past selves crowding in.

She was eight, hiding under the covers with a flashlight and *King of Swords*. The fictional murders and monsters were less frightening than her suddenly bald mother.

She was ten, reading aloud for long hours, with the

occasional correction or explanation from her mom. Her mom's hair was as short as a boy's. It had grown back curly after the chemotherapy.

She was eleven, lying side by side with her once-more bald mom in her parents' bedroom. Trying to help them both escape the pain by slipping into another world.

She was twelve, sitting in a chair next to the hospital bed set up in the living room, reading aloud until her voice cracked. Now her mom found the slightest touch painful, so Bridget could no longer lie next to her. Her mom lay flat on her back, arms and legs so skinny they were barely bumps under the blankets. But her swollen belly was the size of a basketball, filled with fluid her failing liver could no longer process. By now, Bridget was on her fifth time through the books. As she read, she kept checking her mom's yellow-tinged face for the faintest smile of pleasure. Listening for a sigh when a character died. There were no surprises left in the book, no shocks, yet the plots still touched them both.

Those last few weeks of her mom's life, Bridget read to her every free moment. Even when her mom seemed asleep or possibly unconscious, she didn't stop. She was spinning a rope of words, trying to keep her mother anchored to her. An hour after she finished rereading *Court of Sorrows*, the last book then available in the series, her mother slipped from life to death.

Ajay's voice interrupted her thoughts. "But wasn't your mom right? I mean, aren't the books pretty violent? The one episode of the TV show I watched, someone got tortured and another person's head was chopped off." She noticed he didn't mention the scene set in the brothel.

Ajay was right, but also wrong. In the world of Swords and Shadows, people died all the time. But they died for a reason. They didn't die because of something stupid and random like cancer. Although there was no family history, just to be sure, the doctors had tested Bridget's mom for the breast cancer gene, but she didn't have it. While that was good for Bridget, it also meant there was no explanation for her mom's cancer. It had just happened.

In the books, though, not only did death serve a purpose, but it was also portrayed as noble, or at the very least, dramatic. Characters didn't slip away after dwindling for months.

The familiar tightness in her chest made it hard to swallow her bite of taco. "I'm sure a lot went over my head. But the books weren't any scarier than my real life. I ended up reading all of them to my mom."

Bridget had spent hours curled up in bed next to her. She kept her eyes on the page and not on her mother's gaunt face, the bald head she was sometimes too weak to hold up.

"Those books gave us something in common that was better than our real, awful lives. She died right before the last one came out." Giving up on her tacos, Bridget pushed the tray away.

Ajay's mouth twisted. "How old were you?"

"Twelve. The only signing Bob did was at Powell's. I waited in line for seven hours to make sure I could get in."

"Seven *hours*?"

Bridget shrugged. She would have spent the night if she'd had to. Her plan had been to have Haldon sign his latest book and then go to her mom's grave and read it aloud. "It was worth it. But something happened when he was taking questions."

Ajay leaned forward. "What?"

And then Bridget told Ajay the story she'd never shared with anyone except her dad.

BOB

Buffalo

Bob's stomach rumbled. He took stock of the food, all far too healthy. When was the last time he'd eaten a piece of fruit? He couldn't remember. Maybe back when Lilly had been around to urge him on with a smile.

When he first hired Joanne to manage the household, she'd tried in vain to change his habits. He liked crunchy things, fried things, spicy things, and most especially anything salty.

Making the best of his limited choices, Bob now used his teeth to tear open the plastic wrapping on the cheddar cheese. He bit off a corner.

For years, people had been hounding him for *Eyes of the Forest*. They claimed they wanted the end. The answers. They demanded mysteries be unraveled, secrets revealed, King Tristan's killer unmasked.

At least that was what they *said* they wanted, he thought as he chewed.

What they really wanted was a cliffhanger they could obsess over for months. Or a tiny clue the astute could endlessly tweet and Instagram about—or whatever people did these days.

He wasn't a trained monkey who could dance on command, Bob thought, biting off a second cheese corner. He was R. M. Haldon. The author even people who weren't readers now recognized, thanks both to the TV shows and the entertainment media that covered anything popular, even books. His uniform of black T-shirt, stonewashed jeans, and white Nikes made him easily recognizable, but the clincher was the violet silk scarf around his neck. Bob wore it winter and summer, indoors and out. On the rare occasions he washed it, he felt more naked than he did in the shower.

He knew he could always just not wear the scarf, but it was his last tie to Lilly. But thanks to it, Bob could barely walk a block without being stopped and asked for a selfie. Some people didn't even ask, just wrapped their arm around his shoulder or waist, held out their phones, and clicked. All without saying a thing.

Fans said they loved him, but they only loved him for what he could give them. Kobe beef cattle supposedly received daily massages and troughs filled with beer. Classical music was even piped into their stalls.

But they were still destined for slaughter.

Bob couldn't even go out to dinner by himself without someone tweeting or YouTubing about the stains on his shirt or how much he was stuffing his face. So much for being "fans."

The word *fan* was short for *fanatic*. And it wasn't

a new phenomenon. Back in 1844, there'd been mass frenzy at Franz Liszt's concerts, with audience members fighting over the composer's gloves or broken piano strings.

Bob had become public property. It was why he'd hired Joanne. She could grocery shop and run errands and be invisible. That way he didn't have to worry about unflattering photos, tirades about how he wasn't writing fast enough, or the occasional woman (or even man) who thought Bob was sending secret messages of love via his prose.

Every year, he'd become more of a concept than a person. Gained a little more weight. Felt a little more alone. And every year, the number of people who had known him prior to his fame dwindled.

As time passed, Bob's characters became more real to him. But it was one-sided. They couldn't ask about his day. They couldn't talk to him about politics or the playoffs. They didn't care if he was sick. These days, the closest thing Bob had to a friend was Bridget. And he corresponded with her via email.

Nobody much cared what happened to Bob as long as R. M. Haldon produced another book. He needed to finish *Eyes of the Forest*. Everyone agreed on that.

Even Bob.

Only he couldn't.

People didn't believe in writer's block. But it was real. It wasn't that he didn't want to write. He didn't know how to anymore. Every time he thought about shutting down the world he'd created, he froze.

Despite everything he tried, the characters just lay

flat on the page. They didn't get up and walk around any-more, doing surprising things. The ones he'd thought he would kill now seemed too precious to die.

Day after day, he would sit at his computer, deter-mined to write. Instead, he would have a stare-down with the blank screen. On a good day, he might write a few lines, but then minutes later, he would delete them all. Once he'd printed out a few paragraphs, put them aside for a week, and then read them aloud. He'd hoped that would make new words come.

It didn't.

He'd tried taking a walk, taking a bath, taking a nap. Tried outlining, but that was even worse than writing. After reading about an author who wrote with a cap pulled over his eyes, Bob attempted it. But at some point his fingers wandered off the home keys, so it was gibber-ish. He'd tried letting it rest, and he'd tried forcing it. He'd tried writing after a few beers. He'd tried telling himself he could mail-order his favorite chocolate once he finished a chapter. He'd even downloaded a program that showed you images of spiders if you didn't write fast enough but rewarded you with a picture of a kitten for every hundred words you did write.

All he'd seen was spiders.

Eyes of the Forest was going to take as long as it was going to take, Bob thought now as he bit off another hunk of cheese. Everyone was just going to have to deal with that. Including Derrick.

Still chewing, he lay back down, pulled the covers over his head, and fell asleep.

He woke to someone prodding him. Bob rolled over. It was Derrick. Tall. Skinny. Bad skin. That ridiculous wannabe mustache faint on his upper lip.

"Derrick." Relief loosened his tight muscles.

"Hello, Bob." The kid's face was expressionless. He took everything too seriously. Like actually hitting Bob with the butt of the gun, the gun that Bob realized now was obviously fake.

Fun was fun. What had seemed like a good idea after quite a few Bud Lights was now, in the cold winter light of this snowed-in cabin, ridiculous.

"Buffalo." As soon as the word left his lips, Bob relaxed.

But Derrick didn't reach into his pocket and produce the key to the shackles. He just looked at the threatening note, still on top of the typewriter. Then he turned back to stare at Bob, his expression unreadable.

"Buffalo," Bob repeated.

It was the safe word they had agreed upon. Chosen because it wasn't a word Bob or Derrick normally said. It wasn't a word *anyone* normally said. So there was no chance of accidentally using it in conversation. Now its meaning was plain.

It was time to end the charade.

DERRICK

Dangerous Combat Infraction

Derrick stared down at the foolish old man on the bed, the one who'd just said, "Buffalo," as if it mattered. Derrick's note was still propped on the typewriter, undisturbed. The cheese was the only thing that had been touched. It looked like a giant rat had been gnawing at it.

All day, he'd been impatient for school to end. Watching Bridget get in trouble for listening to the audio of *King of Swords*, he'd felt a secret thrill thinking about how soon he would be reading words even she had yet to see. The drive out to the cabin had felt agonizingly slow.

And all that anticipation had been for nothing. His hand tightened on the wand of the stun gun his mom had insisted they get, even though he had no intention of using it. "Why aren't you writing?" he demanded.

Bob pushed himself upright. "Why do you think? Because I probably have a concussion from getting hit in the head." He glared at Derrick. "That definitely wasn't in the plan."

Didn't Bob get that the plan was just a starting point? It was just like in Mysts of Cascadia, the LARP Derrick been playing with his dad a couple of times a month since he was eight years old.

In a LARP, the players and the audience were the same thing. While a plot committee came up with the overarching storylines, it was the player characters, or PCs, who decided how it all actually worked out. PCs had absolute freedom to run headlong into fights, or stay in their cabin all day and talk with other PCs, or anything in between.

"I'm afraid I had to improvise." Hitting Bob with the butt of the heavy plastic gun would have gotten Derrick booted from Cascadia for two "dangerous combat infractions." First, he'd used a weapon (in this case an airsoft gun) that hadn't been safety checked, and second, he'd deliberately struck an illegal area—Bob's head. Anyone who'd met Derrick LARPing, when he played Rickard, the noble leader of the peasant rebellion, would have been shocked by his behavior.

But what was happening now wasn't a game with endless arcane rules. It was real life. And Derrick might just like it better.

"There's a divot in my head." Bob's eyes shone wetly. "I'm probably lucky I woke up at all."

It was clear he'd spent all day lying around having a pity party. Derrick didn't have the patience for it. Not when they had gone to such lengths to help. "I left you a warning. You need to finish *Eyes of the Forest*."

Bob made an obvious effort to change his tone. "Yes, I do," he said brightly, as if to a child. "You're absolutely right. But I've had all day to give this setup some thought. And this idea, as good as it was originally, isn't actually going to work. So I'm telling you again, Derrick." After a meaningful pause, Bob looked him straight in the eye. "Buffalo."

Derrick didn't move.

"I've changed my mind." Bob waved his hand. "It's not that I don't appreciate how you set all this up and even added the treadmill, but the book will get written when the time is right. I can't force it. So I need you to remove the shackles and then take me back home. Of course, you two can keep the ten thousand dollars. I'll even reimburse you for the treadmill. Keep it, sell it, or return it to the store. It doesn't matter."

As if any of that mattered. "You need to finish the series." Derrick had been waiting for years, and he couldn't wait anymore. Wouldn't.

"But I've realized this won't work." Bob offered him a strained smile.

"I'm not doing this for the money. I did it so I could finally read *Eyes of the Forest*. I'm your biggest fan."

Bob sighed. "Don't you get it? That's what everyone says. Literally thousands of people have told me they're my biggest fan."

Anger shot through Derrick. He reflexively raised the stun gun, squeezing the trigger. The air filled with the crackle of electricity. Bob cowered.

He *cowered.*

Bob was afraid of him. Of Derrick. If only people in Cascadia could see their favorite author now.

R. M. Haldon, the guy whose characters would rather die than bow down. And not just die in some simple manner, like by the clean stroke of a headsman's axe, but who would still keep their secrets even if it meant being drawn and quartered. Who would willingly sacrifice themselves for principle. In the Swords and Shadows books, men and women cursed their killers with their last breath. A few even managed to come back from the dead (a tad worse for wear) to wreak revenge.

But as Derrick looked down at the creator of those majestic characters, he realized Bob was really no better than anyone else. The people in grocery stores or Starbucks, the kids Derrick went to school with. Those people wouldn't die for a noble cause. They wouldn't even look up from their phones. It was why Derrick would rather read or LARP. To believe, just for a moment, that things were different.

Bob was an imperfect vessel, but he was still the vessel. "Your words are so much better than you are. You write about heroes when you're nothing but a coward. Do you want me to let you go? Then you have to write."

"But I can't," Bob whined. "Don't you see, Derrick? That's why I came up with this dumb idea in the first place. I have writer's block!"

"That's just a trick your mind is playing on you."

"What do you think I write with, Derrick?" Bob tapped his temple. "With my mind. So if it decides to stop cooperating, I can't do anything about it."

Derrick felt like Queen Jeyne when people didn't take her seriously. They soon learned their mistake. "Oh, I think there are ways to change your mind. Your mind lives inside your body. In fact, it needs your body to exist."

"What do mean?" As Bob shrank back, Derrick felt himself expand. He had found the old man's weakness, and now was the time to exploit it. He'd say anything that would make him write. And hopefully words would be enough.

"Of course, we won't hurt your fingers. We won't hurt your eyes. We won't hurt your head because we need that brain of yours. In fact, I'm sorry I hit you in the head. I got carried away."

"What are you saying?" The old man's voice shook.

"I'm saying that while your mind might need your body, it doesn't necessarily need your *whole* body to write. For example, you don't need your knees or your feet or your ankles to write. You don't need your legs."

"Oh my God." Bob went very, very still.

Derrick saw himself reflected in Bob's shiny eyes. Tall, dark hair, sharp features. He looked far more like one of the heroes in Swords and Shadows than Bob did.

Or maybe he looked more like one of the villains.

But weren't the villains always the most interesting characters?

BOB

A Mask and Gloves

I'll write!" Bob babbled. "I promise!" He made for the treadmill desk.

Derrick's lips thinned. He didn't look convinced. And while the old Bob might have discounted him, today's Bob had woken up to a bloody pillow and a dent on his head. All courtesy of a teenager.

Bob stepped on the treadmill and picked up a piece of paper, trying to calm his racing heart. Talk about a plot twist. Although Bob had created many teenage and even prepubescent characters who were capable of treachery and betrayal, he'd always considered it artistic license.

All the other times he'd interacted with Derrick, the kid had been obsequious. Fawning. He was clearly a far better actor than Bob would have guessed. It must be thanks to his years LARPing in the Mysts of Cascadia.

Because it had to be acting, right? Derrick wouldn't really hurt Bob, would he? He just wanted him to write.

Better start writing Eyes of the Forest. Or else!

Bob set aside the threatening note.

His fan mail had given him the idea. Thanks to the TV show, these days the amount was overwhelming. After an incident with a suspicious white powder that turned out to be talcum, he'd been forced to hire a service to go through it all. Now someone wearing a mask and gloves opened every letter and package before dumping it all in a box and sending it on to Joanne, who then gave it to him.

The box he'd received a couple of months earlier had been typical. Three marriage proposals. A vial of a dark red liquid that appeared to be blood. (Although would the service have allowed it through if it really was?) Four appeals for money. A request he fly to Arkansas to be the surprise guest at a fan's sixtieth birthday party. A dried rose. An urn filled with a dead fan's ashes, accompanied by the request he either eat them or spread them on his grounds. Three baby announcements for children named after characters. A heart-shaped hand-carved wooden box that, to his relief, contained nothing. An ornately framed photo of a woman who harbored the delusion she looked exactly liked Jancy. A handmade white plush unicorn, complete with feathery wings. A mounted plexiglass circle proclaiming Bob had won an award he'd never heard of. A photo of a fresh tattoo of Margarit's name. (Spelled Margrit.)

And among the praise and gifts and appeals had been a postcard with no return address. "Someone should chain you to a typewriter and force you to write *Eyes of the*

Forest." It was a routine disgruntled comment, the kind the service didn't even bother to flag.

But it had sparked the idea. If someone forced him to write, then surely he would.

On paper, this cabin was perfect. It belonged to Derrick's family. There was no cable. No Wi-Fi. No mail service. No close neighbors. And it was winter, so all the summer hikers and bikers would be gone.

It had started out as a fantasy, but the more Bob thought about it, the more real it got. It was, he realized, a genius idea. Once at the cabin, he would have no choice but to write. And so it had all been arranged—Derrick to pretend to fake kidnap him (but not in front of witnesses, lest anyone call the police), the isolated cabin, the old-fashioned typewriter.

Bob had told Derrick not to let him go, no matter what he said. While they'd designated a safe word, he'd planned to never use it.

It had seemed a perfect plan. But clearly Bob hadn't thought about it enough. And he hadn't anticipated them adding their own wrinkles. Like chaining him to a tread-mill instead of a desk. And the food was supposed to be cold pizza, regular Coke, beef jerky, and a variety of flavors of Doritos, Takis, and Kettle Chips.

Now under Derrick's watchful gaze, Bob lined up the edges of the paper with the typewriter. With a clicking sound he turned the knob to move it down and around the roller. He hadn't used a typewriter in decades, but the muscle memory returned without conscious thought.

Derrick was still staring at him, arms crossed. "You need to start the treadmill. Press that green button."

Bob made a face. "I can't write with you watching me. I need to put myself in the scene, and I can't do that when you're just standing there staring at me."

And there was no way he was going to be able to figure out how to free himself if he was being observed.

BRIDGET

Show Some Respect

Despite standing in line seven hours, Bridget had barely managed to snag a seat. For Haldon she'd decided to endure the panicky, trapped feeling being in a crowd sometimes gave her. Many people in the audience were dressed in elaborate costumes, which added to the feeling of unreality. The lady ahead of her was wearing a plastic unicorn horn and wings covered with real feathers. She kept shifting, which meant that in order to see Haldon, Bridget had to constantly alter her own position as well. But she didn't care. She was hearing Haldon himself talk about the book that would soon take her out of her life, make her forget the hole that could never be filled.

After he finished his reading, he took questions from the audience.

The fourth one came from a man dressed like a friar. "Will we ever see more of Nandy Bluestone?" Some of the people around Bridget looked puzzled, but she knew exactly who he was talking about. Nandy Bluestone, a saucy tavern wench, had last been seen flirting with the king in book two. The implication was that even more had transpired between them.

"No comment." Haldon's smile was teasing. "But as I wrote, Nandy does have good childbearing hips . . ."

"No you didn't," Bridget heard herself saying. Too loudly. The room fell silent. Heads turned.

Above his trademark silk scarf, Haldon's features bunched as he focused on her. "What did you say?" He looked angry. But what he'd said had been wrong.

"It's in *Darkest Heart*. You said Nandy Bluestone has narrow hips."

People muttered to each other. The woman ahead of her turned around. The feathers on one wing scratched Bridget's cheek. She waved a finger. "Do you know who you're talking to, child? That is the author himself. Show some respect!"

Bridget's eyes burned with tears. All she'd wanted to do was meet the man who'd made her mom's slow death and her own lonely life bearable, even joyful. And instead she'd made him mad.

Bridget got to her feet. She had to leave. As soon as possible.

A voice boomed over the murmurs of the crowd. It was Haldon. "Can you show me?" From the stacks on the table next to him, he picked up *Darkest Heart* and held it out.

Feeling all eyes on her, Bridget walked toward him. Up close, his signature violet scarf was spotted and his eyes tired. But she didn't read any anger in them. As Bridget took the book, he said, "While she's looking, I'll answer a couple more questions."

Bridget kept her back to the crowd. She didn't know

exactly where the reference was, but she had a visceral feeling as to where to begin. Starting about a third of the way through, she began skimming the text. Haldon was explaining the winged unicorns' social structure when she spotted Nandy's name.

She lifted her head, and Haldon looked over at her. After she pointed at the passage, he took the book from her and read aloud.

When Nandy Bluestone had served the king a haunch of venison, he decided the girl interested him far more than the meal. Nandy was slender as a willow branch, with narrow hips, hair as dark as a crow's wing, and eyes that sparked with mischief. King Tristan, well in his cups, had pulled her onto his lap, saying he was sure she was more tender than the meat. She had not even pretended to protest.

"I think we owe this young lady an apology." Haldon put the book down and started to clap. The rest of the audience joined in. Bridget stared at the tips of her Vans, guessing her face was as red as her hair. She started to return to her seat, but Haldon put his hand on her shoulder.

"Stay. I want to talk to you."

AJAY

A Very Private Person

"W ait." Ajay interrupted Bridget's story. "So you just remembered a single quote from this huge book?" It seemed impossible. "One of six huge books?"

She smiled and shrugged. "It was only four at that point, since I hadn't read the new one yet. And I had read all the other ones a bunch of times."

"Why did Haldon ask you to stay?" From his backpack, he pulled out another waxed cloth bag. This one held cherry tomatoes. He offered some to Bridget, but she waved her hand.

"While he was signing, he asked me questions about the series. I answered every single one."

"That's cool, but why did Haldon care?" Ajay popped a tomato in his mouth, relishing the tang of it. "It's not like there was a trivia contest you could win."

She leaned closer, and his heart did a little hop. "Will you promise not to tell anyone?"

Ajay pinched his finger and thumb together and then ran them across his lips, miming a zipper.

She looked around to make sure no one was paying attention. "He offered me a job."

"A job?" He rocked back in surprise. "Doing what?"

"Keeping track of all the details. Now every time he has a question about what a character looks like, or a family's crest, or a geographic location, or who's descended from whom, he emails me."

"But how do you figure out the answer?"

"I read and reread the books and make searchable notes. It's all in a database I made. So suppose Bob wanted to know what he said about drums in previous books. I could look that up in seconds, and it's all cross-referenced. Like in the second book, he had a character playing a bodhran, which is this Celtic drum made from a goatskin. In the book it's never even actually called a drum. The reader just picks that up from context. But in my database it's listed under drum, as well as the word *bodhran*, and under musical instruments, and under entertainment. It also shows who played it, when, where, and for whom."

Ajay was impressed. "So you're like the continuity supervisor, only for books instead of movies."

"What's a continuity supervisor?"

"Since they shoot movies out of order, the continuity supervisor makes sure that if a guy is wearing a hat in one scene, he's still wearing it in the next."

She tilted her head, her hair swinging. The color was amazing. "How do you know about that?"

"I saw it in the credits, so I googled it. I like those

type of details." He lowered his voice. "So did you sign one of those nondisclosure forms or something?"

"It's not like that." She shook her head. "He's a very private person. I respect that." She took a deep breath. "In fact, you're the only person I've told."

BOB

The Quick Brown Fox

The quick brown fox jumps over the lazy dog, Bob typed. The keys made a scissoring, snapping sound, while his shackles jingled. His hope was the sound would be enough to make Derrick leave him in peace. Leave him long enough to figure his way out of this situation.

Good writing rained trouble down on a character. In the best writing, the trouble was caused by the character's own actions. Which pretty much summed up Bob's current situation.

The quick brown fox jumps over the lazy dog. This time Bob's pinky finger didn't hit the *Q* key hard enough, and the metal arm fell back before it struck the paper. The antique typewriter's black keys required a lot more force than the square white tiles on his little Apple wireless keyboard. At least with the typewriter it was clear how each tap became a letter. His computer keyboard used some wizardry called Bluetooth (a magical name if Bob had ever heard one) to transfer the faint scrabbles and twitches of his fingers into words on an unconnected screen.

How was he going to get out of here? In the past, he'd

put his characters up a metaphorical tree and then waited for them to get themselves down. If it was too easy, he threw some (metaphorical) rocks at them.

Bob had never thought about how frightening it must feel to be high above the ground, trying to duck rocks, with no good solutions.

A bell rang inside the typewriter, making him start. It was a signal he was nearing the edge of the paper. Still mechanically lifting his feet to keep pace with the slowly moving treadmill, Bob swiped the silver bar of the carriage return to the right. Despite everything, he enjoyed the zipping sound it made.

The quick brown fox jumps over the lazy dog. This time there were no mistakes. The clacking of the keys joined the low growl of the motor and the jangle of the shackles. He could hear nothing else. Was Derrick now settled in the living room? Or was he just outside the door, listening?

Bob reviewed his limited choices. If he somehow managed to sever the cable, he could try to break out before Derrick noticed he was gone. Except the window was painted shut. Even if he got outside, hiking back to civilization would be slow going, especially since he would have to avoid roads if he wanted to avoid Derrick. And it would be dark soon. Plus his ankles were chained together, and he didn't have a coat or even shoes. If he was lucky, he would lose toes. If he wasn't, he would lose his life.

Neither option seemed ideal.

Bob found it oddly soothing to be typing the same words, to be slowly walking to nowhere. He tapped the

up arrow on the treadmill and the display changed from
.8 to *.9*. So did that mean he was walking less than a mile
an hour? He pushed the button a few more times until
it read *1.3*. The brisker pace seemed to let his thoughts
move faster. It was also helping him warm up.

The quick brown fox jumps over the lazy dog.

Bob sniffed. He could smell himself. The rancid
stench of terror was now overlaid with the healthier sweat
of a man working out. These days, he didn't go to the
gym. Too many people wanted to get his advice about the
book they were secretly writing (or more often, secretly
only thinking about writing) or tell him they thought a
particular actor on the TV show was ill-suited to the part.
He had an exercise bike at home but never used it.

He reached the end of the page, pulled it free, and
rolled in a new one. *The quick brown fox jumps over the
lazy dog.*

If only he wrote thrillers! Then he would already have
figured out how to get out of here. An intimate familiarity with medieval weaponry was no help in this situation.

Derrick must have a phone. Everyone did these days.
Could he somehow distract him and pilfer it? Then he
could call 911, and they would work their magic and figure out where he was besides some cabin near Mount
Hood.

Only how could he get the phone without Derrick
noticing?

That left physical confrontation. Bob had never been
in a fight of any kind. And while Derrick was scrawny,
he was far younger and more agile than Bob. Bob wasn't

young, mobile, or particularly strong. But he was stubborn, with more than his fair share of guile.

Maybe he could hit Derrick with something. But what? The room didn't offer a lot of choices. The fruit bowl wasn't heavy enough. He was too squeamish to use the half-full chamber pot. That left the typewriter. He hit the treadmill's stop button.

He would invite Derrick to read what he'd written. Imagining the boy bending over the page, he hoisted the typewriter. The effort forced a grunt between his lips. It was heavier than he'd thought. He brought it down on Derrick's imaginary head. Once he did it for real, he would search the unconscious boy for a phone, the key to the shackles, or both. With luck, he would also find the key to the car, so he could drive away and not have to worry about him regaining consciousness before the police showed up.

He set the typewriter back in its original position, turned on the treadmill, and resumed typing. *The quick brown fox jumps over the lazy dog.* Sweat gathered on the small of his back as he typed and walked and waited.

Finally, he heard the hinges creak. Turning to look, Bob nearly lost his balance.

"I've been productive," he said jovially. "Want to see what I've come up with?"

Derrick came closer. Bob hit the OFF button for the treadmill. In the sudden silence, his breathing sounded too loud, too fast. Would it give him away? Maybe Derrick would chalk it up to him being out of shape.

The boy stopped a few feet away. Not close enough

for Bob to bean. But perhaps, he feared, close enough to read what he'd typed.

Derrick pointed up at the ceiling. "You really think I'd leave you alone?"

Bob followed his finger. And then he spotted it. Black, round, not much bigger than a car fob. It blended in with the knotholes, but it was a tiny spy camera.

Pointed at him.

DERRICK

Non-Player Character

Sitting in the back row of Introduction to Economics, Derrick surreptitiously checked his phone for the dozenth time. On it was the video feed of what he now thought of as the Haldon Cam. Bob was typing steadily, as he had been every time Derrick checked. It was such a temptation to ditch school, drive back to the cabin, and immediately read what he'd written. To finally return to Derrick's beloved world of Swords and Shadows.

But he forced himself to wait. Reading only a few hundred words would just whet his appetite. Would remind him of how long he'd been starving.

Away from school, Derrick was usually at a LARP or preparing for one: sewing new garb, crafting weapons, and working on plotlines. Mostly in his room, because his mom was not a big fan. Joanne thought fantasy in general and LARPing in particular was a waste of time, a way to avoid real life, and a time suck. And that was when she was being charitable.

Earlier in the year, his mom had unexpectedly found herself out of a job. Her then-employer, a model turned actress, had impulsively shaved her head and jetted off to the Himalayas, planning to meditate for a year.

In Portland, openings for full-time personal assistants were rare. Then his mom got lucky. Her agency got a new client, an author who was finding it increasingly taxing to venture out in public. It would be easy work—simple cooking, cleaning, and errand running. The author never entertained and liked to make his own travel arrangements. His mom was warned that he did have lots of overzealous fans, but she was used to them from previous jobs.

But when she learned it was R. M. Haldon, his mom almost turned it down. She blamed two men for her divorce. One was Derrick's dad, Curtis. The other was Haldon. Over two decades ago, Curtis had been one of the first fans of *King of Swords*, a new fantasy by an unknown local author. He became so obsessed he started a LARP inspired by it.

In Joanne's view, both Curtis and Bob were pathetic. Grown men who cared about unicorns and magic, when the real world had neither.

After his mom finally told Derrick the name of her new employer, she refused to introduce him, no matter how much he begged. To appease him, she eventually gave him one of Bob's many fantasy con T-shirts.

Derrick delighted in owning something that had belonged to his idol. And then econ class gave him an idea. Why not take advantage of his mom's access to Bob, or more precisely, Bob's stuff? From class, he knew that demand was either elastic—increasing if something was cheap, and decreasing if it was expensive—or inelastic, meaning price had little effect on demand.

And the demand for memorabilia was very much inelastic. Fans would pay a lot for something a star had touched. Enterprising folks had sold Justin Timberlake's unfinished French toast, Scarlett Johannson's used tissue, William Shatner's kidney stone, Britney Spears's chewed gum. One quick thinker who happened upon Brad Pitt and Angelina Jolie had even sold a jar he'd opened and closed in their vicinity. The eBay listing claimed it probably contained a molecule of air that had made direct contact with at least one of them. It sold for more than $525.

R. M. Haldon memorabilia was a popular search term on Google, but all Derrick could find were various types of paper Bob had signed: books, scripts, the odd poster. A signed first edition was easily worth a thousand.

If only there was something more for fans to buy.

So Derrick decided to give it to them. But not on eBay, where questions might be raised. Instead, he turned to the dark web, the internet's evil twin, a place he'd already done some exploring. With enough Bitcoin, you could buy anything there. Netflix accounts. Uranium. Credit card numbers. Grenade launchers. Fake passports. Usernames and passwords. Even a hit man.

Derrick began with one of Bob's signature black T-shirts that his mom diverted from the wash to her purse. He put it up for sale, complete with a photo Joanne had surreptitiously taken of Bob wearing it. The same distinctive tomato sauce stain was on the chest in both. Listed at the equivalent of five hundred dollars in Bitcoin, it sold in less than three hours. After that, every few days Derrick posted something else his mom had brought home. A toothbrush. A pillowcase. Even Bob's hair clippings.

He switched to auction-type sales. The money was better, and people tended to get competitive, especially for one-of-a-kind items.

Selling bits and pieces of Bob's ordinary, boring life hadn't slaked Derrick's desire to meet the great man himself. And finally his mom had asked to let Derrick come to the house.

The night before, Derrick had been unable to sleep. Perhaps he could share some of the ideas he'd come up with while working on the plot committee for Mysts of Cascadia. Maybe Haldon would even offer a sneak peek at *Eyes of the Forest*.

The next day, he trembled as he stepped into Haldon's magnificent office. Derrick was thankful he'd thought to set his phone to record and put it in his shirt pocket, because it was impossible to take everything in. His mom had complained about how hard it was to dust, but her words hadn't conveyed the wonder of it all. One wall was crowded with framed awards, antique illustrated maps, and wicked-looking swords. The other wall was dedicated to hundreds of shelves holding two-inch-high figurines.

In the back right corner stood a full suit of armor that Derrick was pretty certain was actually from the Middle Ages. In the back left corner was a giant boxy silver robot, like from a 1950s sci-fi movie. Draped around its shoulders was a purple velvet cloak.

Sandwiched between the armor and the robot was a huge battered wooden desk the size of a twin bed. Every inch of the desktop was covered. Derrick's eyes skittered over a crystal ball, a feather quill, a stuffed raven, a jade figure of a dragon, and a two-foot-tall black rock cut in half to reveal purple and white crystals within.

Dominating them all was a huge Mac desktop with a bigger display than their TV at home. On it was not a page of *Eyes of the Forest*, but a frozen image he recognized from a Jim Carrey movie. Not one of the good ones, either.

And sitting in a leather overstuffed chair was the man himself. He looked just like the thousand pictures Derrick had seen. Black T-shirt, light jeans, old-school Nikes too broken down to be cool. And wrapped around his neck was his trademark violet scarf.

With a movement of his chin, he indicated Derrick should approach.

Closer to, Haldon's face was flushed. Crumbs speckled the scarf and T-shirt.

Derrick was trembling so hard he thought he might fly apart. How many times had he read Haldon's books, looking for clues to his alter ego, Rowan/Rickard, the peasants' leader? As Rowan grew from a boy to a man in the books, Derrick's Rickard had also grown in importance. Thanks to them, in Cascadia Derrick had been able to re-create himself as everything he was not in real life. Derrick was book smart, but Rickard was clever. Derrick wasn't brave, but Rickard was never afraid, even if he should be. And while Derrick was practically invisible, whenever he played Rickard, people looked to him for guidance.

R. M. Haldon stuck out a big, square paw. Derrick was almost afraid to shake it. What if he squeezed too hard and somehow damaged his hand?

"Oh, it's so wonderful to meet you, Mr. Haldon," he babbled, gently grasping the outstretched fingers, which seemed oddly gritty. "I'm your biggest fan."

Had Haldon rolled his eyes? Surely not.

The other man pulled back his hand and stuck it in the open bag of Doritos on his lap. "Okay, kid, thanks, but you don't need to say that stuff. And just call me Bob."

"But it's true." Derrick's voice was weak. "I love your books." The bright colors in the room were dimming.

Haldon shrugged. "That's what everyone says. No one is ever my number two fan, or my number one thousand fifty-third fan. And they always say it like I owe them something." He shoved a handful of chips into his mouth.

Shame washed over Derrick. He'd been stupid enough to think he would make an impression. Maybe even make a friend.

Haldon listed a little to one side, then righted himself, leaving behind a ghostly orange handprint on the chair's arm. Derrick refocused on the cluttered desk behind him. Among the detritus were at least a dozen crumpled silver cans.

It all became clear. Derrick had seen his grandpa drunk often enough to recognize the signs. The slurred words. The swaying. The unfocused eyes. The meanness.

Derrick found his own meanness. Instinctively, he knew how to hurt Haldon most.

"Do you think you're going to still have fans if you never finish *Eyes of the Forest*? There's a dozen writers now who write the same kind of books you do—and they're publishing."

Haldon closed his eyes, and a long moment passed. "You think I don't want to write it, kid?" His eyes were still closed. His voice was soft. "Do you think it's easy sitting here day after day, trying to make the words appear? Do you think I like getting letters from fans threatening to chain me to a typewriter?"

And suddenly Derrick knew how to help. Not for Haldon's sake, but for the books' sake. The books were bigger than Haldon. Bigger than anything.

"Maybe that fan is right," he said.

Haldon snorted. Still, he opened his bleary eyes. "What?"

"What if you really were chained to a typewriter? What if the only way to get free was to finish? But not here. Here you've got all your toys." Derrick pointed at Jim Carrey, frozen mid-gape. "All your distractions. But I know the perfect place."

That was how it all began.

BOB

Added Up to Nothing

B ob kept his fingers moving over the keys as he end-lessly stepped forward. But just like his steps, his words added up to nothing. All they did was delay Derrick's return. The spy camera would see Bob typing, but not the actual words.

> *In front of me squats the typewriter. The empty page stares at me, unblinking. I need a shower. I slept poorly last night. I pleaded with Derrick for coffee, but he brought none. He demanded my email password in return for a visit to the toilet.*

> *Now I realize how shortsighted I was to give it up. Anyone who expresses concern will be met with a lie. People know I don't answer my phone, so that won't worry them. With email, Derrick will be like a Skin Changer, only via technology instead of magic. Although what is magic but that which we don't yet understand?*

And who would even be concerned? Jamie would just think Bob was avoiding him, as he had for months. Frank, Bob's agent, who had been with him from the beginning, knew he didn't like to be bothered unless it was vital. As a result, Frank just sent him the occasional round-up of new foreign deals to increasingly smaller, more obscure countries.

This morning had been humiliating, first the begging (Bob refused to poop in the chamber pot) and then shuffling down the hall, his chain clanking. The boy had allowed him to close the door. Inside, the only window was a glazed square too small for even a child to squeeze through. The medicine cabinet and drawers held just a tube of toothpaste and three toothbrushes, one still in its wrapper. In the shower, a bottle of shampoo and a bar of soap. Nothing Bob could repurpose. In movies, prisoners turned toothbrushes into shivs, but they had concrete to sharpen them on.

After being shackled to the desk again, Bob had tried writing *Eyes of the Forest* as ordered but hadn't been able to complete even a sentence. Now he was freewriting. There were few rules in freewriting, mostly just not stopping. Even if he only typed *I don't know what to write* over and over, it would still be freewriting. No worries about grammar, word choice, subject-verb agreement, or even typos. He'd already had to let that last one go. No COMMAND-Z on a typewriter.

At a minimum, freewriting might get out some of the sludge filling his head. Then with luck, he'd actually write something decent. Some of Bob's best characters, his most surprising images had come from freewriting.

But that had been when he was writing the first book or two. The pressure to make *Eyes of the Forest* perfect had paralyzed him. Freewriting no longer felt serious enough. Productive enough.

The last time he'd tried to freewrite, Bob had given up after a few minutes, with no consequences. Now he couldn't.

Freewriting was like a singer warming up by singing scales. If Bob just kept typing, if he pushed back the weight of inertia and fear, then maybe he would find his way to the book. Or at least an indelible image. An unexpected character. A fresh simile.

He'd been stuck long before he met Derrick. It had been painful, but at least it hadn't been life threatening. The writer Samuel Johnson had said the prospect of hanging concentrated the mind wonderfully, but the prospect of being maimed did not seem to be having the same effect on Bob.

There is too much of me. My thighs chafe from pushing past each other. My breaths leave my mouth like faint smoke. I wonder how many breaths I have left.

Less thinking. More writing. I miss my characters. Or do I? Maybe I miss life.

Even as a child, Bob had been odd and lonely. He had a freakish imagination and no ready outlet for it. His parents were always after him to "go outside and play with your friends," when he had no friends or interest in the outdoors. Instead, he had collected Lego figures, giving them all names, elaborate backstories, and current conflicts. His first true friend had been Lilly, who he had met playing Dungeons and Dragons in college.

This cabin is a prison, and this room a cell within it. Or have I been my own prison?

When Bob started writing as an adult, he hadn't

known how to, but it hadn't mattered. After Lilly left him, writing had been a way to fill up the empty evening and weekend hours. If his life was featureless and gray, then he would create a fantasy that was anything but. The first book had taken three years to write and two to sell, and then just for twelve thousand dollars. But before it was even published, the reviews were rapturous.

The words won't come. They are hiding. My fingers punch the keys anyway.

The common wisdom was that writers were either planners or pantsers—people who wrote by the seat of their pants. Bob was a pantser. People refused to believe it. How could he have created all those different lands and people and magic without planning? They didn't understand that thinking up details was effortless. It was keeping them straight later that was hard.

In the beginning it had been easy to take Swords and Shadows in surprising new directions. Bob enjoyed choreographing elaborate fight scenes, coming up with grisly new ways for characters to die, and creating love triangles where each side seemed equally worthy. Whenever he got bored with existing characters and plotlines, he added new supernatural powers and creatures. For the most part, he invented his own mythology. It wasn't like there was a flying unicorn he could interview. But the world he'd created was so big that Bob could no longer keep it all in his head.

Then Bridget had shown up, the answer to all his problems.

I can still see Bridget trembling at Powell's. Just a skinny little kid with milk-pale skin and russet hair. But when she spoke about the books, it was clear she was a savant. She was a walking encyclopedia of the world I had created, effortlessly remembering details I had just thrown out there over the years.

And then I learned about her dead mother. Such an echo of my own life. I know what it's like to feel abandoned and alone.

A muffled thump outside his window made Bob jerk, adrenaline running down his spine like an electric shock. But it was just a tree branch that had bent under the weight of falling flakes until it finally flexed far enough to spring back, shaking the snow free.

Maybe he could learn from it. Derrick wanted a book, but who said it had to be the real *Eyes of the Forest*? Maybe all Bob needed to do was to write something, anything, and pretend it was the book. Then he would bide his time, looking for the right moment to break free.

BRIDGET

Like in Real Life

When Bridget walked into physics class, her heart gave a little leap at the sight of Ajay. He offered her a crooked smile as she slid into her seat.

She took a deep breath, glad there was no one near them. "I brought you something." Sliding her backpack off her shoulder, she unzipped it.

"What?"

Before Bridget could lose her courage, she handed over her copy of *King of Swords*. This would be the first time she had loaned it out. It wasn't that she was a collector. Collectors prided themselves in owning books that hadn't been read, but that certainly wasn't true of her copy. It was far from pristine. Instead of being wrapped in clear protective plastic, the cover was faded and tattered. Inside, a couple of pages were spotted from an unfortunate incident involving peanut butter–chocolate chip cookie dough.

Ajay took it gingerly, almost reverently. "This looks well loved."

Bridget's shoulders loosened. "Just trying to get someone else to join the cult."

Looking uncomfortable, he extended the book back toward her. "I know how much it means to you. I don't feel right taking it."

She blinked in surprise. "Oh, no, I just meant you could borrow it. You know, read and return. You're right that I wouldn't want to part with it. But I will loan it out."

Ajay turned the book on its side. "It's not as thick as some of them."

"Yeah, each book has gotten a little bigger."

He tilted his head. "Can I ask you a favor?"

"Sure." Her heart was already beating faster.

"Could you maybe read it to me?"

Joy bloomed in her chest. The bell rang before she could answer. As Mr. Manning started to speak, she mouthed, "Yes."

Class passed in a blur. Last night, all she had been able to think about was her lunch with Ajay. What she'd said. What he'd said. How he'd looked when he asked questions or listened. The taste of the food, and the fact that he'd cooked it.

And now it seemed like he wanted to spend even more time with her. To do that, she would be happy to read him anything, up to and including one of those old telephone books like her grandma had. But this? When she had made the decision to loan Ajay the book, the most she had hoped for was being able to discuss it with him later.

When the bell rang, Bridget realized she hadn't heard a thing Mr. Manning had said. She was just lucky he hadn't asked her anything.

As they got up, Derrick called from the back of the

room. "Hey, Bridget. Wait up. I want to ask you something."

She and Ajay exchanged a glance. Then he said something she didn't quite catch and made for the door.

Had he said he was going to wait for her? Or maybe that he wasn't? Whatever he'd said, he was already disappearing into the roar and bustle of the hall. Today was Halloween, and there was a certain energy in the air. A few of the girls were even wearing costumes, walking the fine line between sexy and too sexy for school.

Bridget was so wrapped up in thinking about Ajay that Derrick's voice made her start.

He loomed over her, thin and slightly stooped, like a parenthesis. The height was new and still awkward. "Hey, Bridget. I just wanted to say I love those books, too. Swords and Shadows. They're epic."

This was no secret. Who could forget Costume Day in fifth grade, almost exactly six years ago? Certainly not their classmates. It was held the day before or after Halloween so that the school district couldn't be accused of celebrating a pagan holiday. Derrick had come dressed as Rowan, complete with a red cloak and flowery speech. But that was before the TV show, before most middle schoolers had any kind of familiarity with the world of Swords and Shadows. Bridget had been the only one who hadn't thought Derrick was a pint-sized Prince Charming. Even then, it wasn't the outfit or the language that had branded Derrick as an übernerd. It was the complete seriousness he'd brought to the role. He had been all too solemn, like someone cast as Jesus Christ in a Passion play, who felt it was blasphemy to act un-Christlike, even off stage. Any teasing had made him flush and then get angry.

So of course the other kids had teased him unmercifully.

Even now, as Wyatt walked by, he fake-coughed the word "Nerds!"

"Yes," Bridget said, ignoring Wyatt and wishing she could ignore Derrick. "The books are amazing." Was Ajay waiting for her?

"Have you been to one of Haldon's readings? Do you ever wonder what he's like in real life?"

Even though Bridget was only half-listening, she had the strangest feeling that Derrick was suppressing some strong emotion. For a second, she focused on him. While nobody looked good under fluorescent lights, Derrick had the kind of skin that cruel kids sometimes called pizza face. But now a smile was playing about his lips.

Oh no. She got it. Derrick must like her. Like her the way she liked Ajay. *Oh no. No, no, no.*

"I more just think about the books," she said truthfully. "Not the author." As she spoke, she realized how little she really knew about Bob. Then again, all he ever wanted to communicate about was the world of the books. She snuck another glance toward the hall. She was relieved to spot Ajay, but that relief was short-lived when she saw that a senior girl sporting cat ears, a fur tail, and a tight black sweater was talking to him.

Derrick made an impatient noise. "Don't you ever wish that you could read that last book, like, right now?"

"B—Haldon will write it when he writes it." Bridget was so distracted that she almost forgot her connection with Bob was a secret.

Derrick smiled at her again, but this time it was more of a smirk. "I'm hoping someone will help him realize how important that is to his fans."

Bridget looked at Derrick now, really looked. Was there any chance that he knew who she was? Had he read that one fan publication she'd let interview her? But it was nearly a zine, one step up from being photocopied at Kinko's. Besides, she'd only used her first name.

Then Ajay motioned to her from the hall, and every other thought vanished. "I'm sorry," she said to Derrick, no longer really seeing him, "but I need to get to lunch."

DERRICK

The Dark Side

Derrick didn't let himself chuckle until Bridget was out in the hall. She clearly had no idea, none, of what was happening to Bob. She hadn't been concerned at all. Her face had been as placid as a pail of milk.

He had figured out who Bridget really was in late September. His mom had repeated an offhand comment Bob once made about his researcher, and that had been enough to start Derrick digging.

He'd initially pictured the researcher as a female version of Bob: an overweight woman in her sixties. It was a shock when he realized she was really the quiet redhead in his physics class. While he had never spoken to her before today, the last few months he had watched her from the back of the room. Sometimes he daydreamed about how she would make an excellent Cascadian elf. It was so easy to imagine her clad in a short green dress, laced tightly at the bodice and worn with black tights, black leather greaves, and over-the-knee black boots, with the tips of fake ears just poking out through her hair.

And now he had dared to walk right up to the line. To dance on the knife's edge. Yet it was clear she was none the wiser. In the past, Derrick had pulled off a few similar tricks in Cascadia, convinced others he was friend instead of foe or vice versa, but this was a new level of sophistication.

Now he watched Bridget go off with that Ajay. When he'd seen Bridget slip *King of Swords* to Ajay, jealousy had pinched him. Wasting a book on someone like Ajay. At least he wasn't a sports guy, but even though he got good grades, he definitely wasn't a book guy. He more liked to talk about something boring. So boring Derrick couldn't remember it at first. Cooking, that was it. Another activity, like LARPing, that mostly interested adults, yet no one made fun of Ajay for it.

Derrick told himself he didn't care. And in a few hours he would be reading something even Bridget hadn't.

As soon as school let out, Derrick drove out to the cabin, driving a little too fast even once he got on the barely plowed roads. Once he unlocked the door, he made a beeline for Bob's room. The old man let out a surprised *huh* as Derrick made straight for the stack of paper. He turned it over to read the first page.

In front of me squats the typewriter. The empty page stares at me, unblinking. I need a shower.

Derrick looked up. "What *is* this crap?"

Bob pushed the OFF button and the treadmill slowed to a stop. Now the room was silent except for the sound of his breathing. He looked sweaty. And he smelled.

And this was the guy Derrick used to venerate?

"You can't expect me to just start pounding out a story," Bob said. "I'm trying to write my way to it."

Anger bloomed hot in Derrick's chest. "I've given you everything you said you needed to write. And I warned you about the consequences. But instead of writing, you're typing your stupid, ordinary, boring thoughts no one cares about."

"I gave you guys the money. Just let me go."

"Not until *Eyes of the Forest* is done."

Bob made a scoffing noise. "All this so you can read some book?"

Derrick gritted his teeth. Why had the muse chosen such an imperfect vessel? Bob didn't even respect his own creation. "First of all, it's not just some book," he said with every ounce of patience he could muster. "And second of all, don't you get it? It's not just about me being able to read it. You had your plan. We had ours. In some ways, they're the exact same plan."

The old man tilted his head. "What do you mean?"

"You want to finish your book. We want the same thing. And then we'll sell it."

"My publisher already paid for half of it." Bob brightened. "But if you let me go, I'll give you the other half."

"No." Derrick tapped his chest. "We're going to sell it. Ourselves."

"But that's what my publisher does. I don't think they'll look too kindly on anyone trying to make an end run around them."

"Not in bookstores. On the dark web."

Bob went silent. It was a good feeling, making him shut up. He closed his eyes, exhaled through his nose, opened them again. "You're not serious."

"There are a lot of people who would give anything to read *Eyes of the Forest*. Pay almost anything."

"Once I finish, the series is over. I'm not sure my readers really want that."

Derrick heard the hidden truth. "You mean *you* don't want that. But your readers? They want answers. One of the most popular threads on Reddit is just people speculating about the ending."

"And there are countless blogs and parody Twitter accounts and articles. Some scholarly. So?"

"So a lot of those people would be willing to take a quick trip to the dark side if it meant they didn't have to wait any longer."

"They wouldn't do that." Bob sounded like he was trying to convince himself.

Derrick couldn't help smiling. "You don't think so? They're so desperate, so invested in you as the maker of Swords and Shadows, that they're even willing to buy anything you've touched."

"What do you mean?" Bob rubbed his stubbly cheeks with one hand.

"They just want to be close to you. And if they can't read the book, maybe the next best thing would be to sleep in your sheets. Wear your old socks."

The old man's mouth fell open. "You're going to sell my personal belongings?"

Pride spread a smile over Derrick's face. "We already have. For the past three months."

"My old socks?" Bob made a face. "What's to stop you from just saying they're mine?"

"I created a certificate of authenticity, complete with an official-looking seal. Plus each piece comes with a picture of you using the item in question."

"Wait—you said my sheets. Joanne's been taking pictures of me sleeping?" Stepping off the treadmill desk, he sat heavily on the bed.

Derrick shrugged. "It's not hard. She said you sleep a lot."

"Is that where my favorite argyle socks went? And that little statue of a gryphon that used to be on my desk?"

Derrick let his silence answer.

"No wonder I couldn't find my Blazers cap the other day. I was like, I know I put it down here. Where can a hat go?"

Derrick smiled. "It sold for north of six thousand."

Bob's mouth fell open. "Six thousand dollars for a hat?"

"You know what would really go for a lot?" Derrick reached out to finger the scarf. "This is iconic. It's how everyone recognizes you."

Bob jerked away. He had paled, but also set his jaw. "The only way you're taking it off me is if I'm dead."

Derrick shrugged. "Okay, so not the scarf." In his head, he put an asterisk after the sentence, and then the word *yet.* "As for the book, we're going to sell it chapter by chapter. At a hundred bucks a pop."

"For a single chapter?" Bob scoffed. "That's more than three times what the entire book will cost when it comes out. Why would anyone pay that?"

"Because no one believes the whole book's ever going

to appear. It's years overdue. They'll figure it's better to get some chapters now, even if they're expensive, than to get zero chapters forever."

"But that's a lot of money for a few pages."

"You don't understand. There are hundreds of people just like me out there. Thousands."

Bob cocked his head. "Once you sell a chapter to someone, how will you stop them from turning around and selling it to someone else?"

"We'll sell it as a PDF and disable the copy-paste and print features."

"You really think that will work?" Bob snorted. "My publisher has a whole team devoted to book piracy. There's no way to stop someone from screenshotting it page-by-page. Run the screenshots through an optical character reader, and they'll have it back again, more or less. I've seen some crazy mistakes creep in that way, but all the pirates say sharing is caring."

"We'll get the biggest fans before anyone else. They don't even want to wait another day. Not if they can read it now."

AJAY

A Bridge Too Far

"You outdid yourself, Ajay," his grandmother said, taking a bite of halwa. The dessert's orange color was set off perfectly by the topping of bright green chopped pistachios.

"Everything was delicious," his grandfather agreed.

Ajay had spent weeks preparing for tonight's Diwali celebration. At school nearly everyone else had been preoccupied with thoughts of Halloween, which this year coincided with Diwali, or the Festival of Light. In many ways, Halloween, with its emphasis on death, was antithetical to the spirit of Diwali. (When he was little, his parents had always tried to find a balance, decorating with jack-o'-lanterns instead of ghosts and ghouls and steering him away from all-black costumes.) While the stories of Diwali varied depending on what part of India you were from, all had a common thread—marking the victory of good over evil, light over dark. It was one of the biggest holidays on the Hindu calendar, as import-ant as Christmas to Christians.

Diwali meant feasting. New clothes. Decorating the house with strings of twinkling lights and painted diya—clay lamps. Like every year, his mom had created a rangoli at the end of the driveway, filling the design of an oil lamp surrounded with flower petals with bright red, green, purple, and pink sand. After dinner, they would go outside and light sparklers.

To celebrate the occasion, most of Ajay's extended family was here. His older sister, Aprita, home from medical school. His three living grandparents. Papa's brother and his wife and two little girls. Later they would Face-Time with Mama's sister's family in Seattle.

On the buffet table, the white platters that had been overflowing with sweet and savory foods were now nearly empty. For the past few weeks, Ajay had spent every free moment cooking. Some days the kitchen had been filled with the delicate scents of milk and rose essence blending together, and others it had carried the savory smell of freshly ground spices. He had made a traditional meal of lentils, veggies, samosas, and roti. But the mithai, the sweets, were the best part of the meal, and it was those he had labored over the most. In addition to the halwa, he had made kheer (a rice pudding), gulab jamun (like donut holes in a sweet syrup), and sweet shankarpali (bite-sized deep-fried sugar cookies).

Even though Ajay was 100 percent Indian-American, his background was a bit of a hodgepodge. All four of his grandparents had come from different parts of India, which meant they all spoke different local languages. His other grandmother, who had died last year, hadn't spoken Hindi at all.

"Aprita, there is a boy we think you should meet," his grandmother said now.

His parents stiffened and exchanged a glance as Grandmother fumbled with her phone. She finally pulled up a man's photo and reached across the table. His sister took it gingerly and then, after a glance, gave it back.

"Don't go by the picture photo," Grandmother said quickly. "He is a very nice boy. Good family. I'm just saying you should meet him, that's all."

Aprita kept her eyes on her lap. "I'm too busy with my studies."

Grandmother was not deterred. "And soon you'll be a resident. Your mother followed the same path and managed to find time to meet your father." They had been engaged a month after that first meeting. "You're not getting any younger. And this boy would be perfect for you."

"Look, Mama," Ajay's father finally said. "America will always be the world's melting pot. It's why you and Papa came here in the seventies. It's why we decided to raise our family to honor the traditions of India as well as to embrace American customs. The children were born here, and their future is here. They're more American than not."

His father's father spoke up. "They are also Indian. America won't let them forget that. So why should we turn our back on that truth?"

Breaking the uncomfortable silence that followed, his mother got up and began to clear the dishes.

~

Later, there was a knock on Ajay's door.

"Come in," he said.

It was his sister. Aprita perched on the edge of his bed, smoothing her new red and gold sari. He had complimented her on it earlier.

"Tonight was your night, wasn't it?" Her voice was tinged with bitterness.

"What do you mean?" Although he had an idea.

"'Oh, Ajay is such a marvelous cook!' You don't even see how lucky you are. How free. If you hadn't had me paving the way, your life would be so much different. I had to fight for things you take for granted. And then of course you're the boy and can get away with more."

If anything, Ajay should have been the one filled with resentment for how his parents and especially his grandparents insisted on holding Aprita up as an example. He said, "I don't think I have it easy. If I come home with a ninety-five percent, it's not 'You did a good job,' but 'Why did you miss five points?' They're always talking about how much better your grades were and how you were valedictorian and a finalist in the 3M Young Scientist Challenge in eighth grade."

She made a scoffing noise. "And do you think that was easy? They've been guiding me down this path since I was a baby. Their plan was always for me to be a doctor. You know they even put Mom's old stethoscope in my crib."

"Do you not want to be one?" Ajay asked, suddenly concerned. He put his hand on her wrist.

"Luckily, I do. I just wish I could have made my own choices. You're a boy, but they let you cook and think it's adorable, even though our grandmothers were expected to be responsible for everything in the kitchen." She sighed. "When I was in high school, all I was allowed were my studies and my chores." She pronounced it *ishtudies,* the way their grandparents would. "Everything else was irrelevant. I wanted to learn how to play the guitar, but of course they insisted on it being the violin. You have so much more freedom than I ever did."

"I didn't get to pick my birth order," he said mildly.

"And now Grandmother wants to arrange a marriage for me."

"You know Mama and Papa will never make you do that."

"You're right. They just expect me to marry an Indian-American man."

Ajay decided to risk it. "How do you think they would feel if I had a girlfriend? Not that I'm saying I do. It's just a hypothetical."

By the look Aprita gave him, he knew she wasn't fooled by his "hypothetical" question. She did a passable imitation of their grandfather. "Don't waste your time on such useless matters. Your job is to study and become successful in your career. We didn't come to this country so that you can worry about friends and love and whatnot." Then she added in her own voice, "Dating is an American thing."

"But we *are* Americans, like Papa said. We've never even been to India. We don't even know much Hindi. And like he said, America's a melting pot."

"They only want you to melt so much, Ajay. You need

to think with your head and not your heart." Her gaze softened. "What's her name?"

"Bridget." Her name was as sweet as palm jaggery in his mouth.

Her eyes narrowed. "A white girl? That may be a bridge—or should I say, Bridget?—too far."

his mouth.

BOB

In the Nick of Time

Rugged and rocky was the coastline. The weather-beaten trail twisted back and forth through the barren land. Overhead, the relentless sun rained down its luminous rays on the man struggling forward. Little did Rowan know that this was actually the calm before the storm.

Yesterday, after his stolen mount had fallen to its knees and then been unable to rise, Rowan had slit its throat. It had been a mercy, and not just for the horse. After catching the hot, salty blood in his hands, he had slurped it up, the only food or drink he'd had in days.

But that was yesterday. Now his tongue was so swollen it filled his mouth.

The pounding waves masked the sound of his pursuers. He did not hear them until they were nearly upon him, astride three heaving mounts. Spinning around, Rowan barely had time to reach back and draw the swords from the crossed sheaths on his back.

"Prepare to embrace your creator in the haunts of hell, peasant!" thundered the leading soldier.

"First you must kiss my blade, wretch!" In the

nick of time, Rowan parried the soldier's lance with one sword while his second cut a new, red smile on his attacker's face.

Screaming with his smaller, original mouth, the mercenary crumpled from his saddle, sprinkling the parched earth with scarlet droplets.

The second soldier spurred his steed toward Rowan. "Damn you, you miscreant serf!" he shrieked, riding over his dying companion. His muscular right arm thrust a flashing steel blade at Rowan's unprotected neck—

Just as Rowan launched himself with his characteristic catlike grace, not backward, but forward. The second soldier's sword met only empty air. As Rowan leapt, he sheathed his own blade in the other man's vital organs. The soldier emitted a groan as he tumbled from his steed, disturbing the golden sands of what would soon be his deathbed.

Cool as a cucumber, Rowan turned toward the lone surviving mercenary. With a grin, he tossed his remaining sword from left hand to right.

The man saw the writing on the wall. Putting the spur to his mount's sides, he tried to swivel about to return whence he came.

But his steed's four hooves were no match for Rowan's two swift feet. And soon Rowan's scarlet-streaked blade found a new home.

Bob found himself grinning as his fingers danced over the keys. The writing was terrible, which was perfect.

All he needed to do was write something, anything, and tell Derrick it was *Eyes of the Forest*. The boy seemed a bit simple, so it wouldn't be hard to convince him.

Letting go had allowed Bob to write two pages in less than twenty minutes. He'd just starting plunking away. It helped that he was alone. Derrick had gotten up early to drive to school. After taking Bob to the bathroom, he had replenished the pile of healthy food. Before leaving, he had reminded Bob how important it was to write. Really write.

This was the result.

Why was Rowan on the coast? What coast? Who had hired the soldiers chasing him? How had he managed to escape the blade aimed at his throat? When had his speech gotten so flowery? Bob had no idea about any of it, but he'd danced on the edge of the precipice before. It reminded him of writing *King of Swords*, which had almost been an out-of-body experience, as if he was taking dictation. And this time, he probably wouldn't need to smooth the edges down until all the pieces fit together.

Suddenly it all seemed so easy. It might come down to how fast he could type. Bob thought he typed about forty words per minute. That was—he multiplied in his head— twenty-four hundred words an hour. And what else was there to do in this room? He could easily write eight hours a day, or about twenty thousand words. His last book had been one hundred fifty thousand words. Theoretically, in a little more than a week, Derrick would be turning him loose.

But now that Bob's fingers were no longer moving, reality sank in. Thinking he could write an entire book in a week was the kind of math he did whenever he stepped on the scale and found that for some unknown reason, he'd lost a pound. In a single day, a whole pound had just disappeared! Giddy, Bob would immediately start projecting. In a week, he could be down seven. If he kept it up, soon he would be at his goal weight. Never again would his doctor make those faces about his spare tire.

But of course it never worked like that. The next day Bob would actually be back to his old weight or even above it, his "loss" erased.

Still, even if it took him weeks, this was a way forward, one a typewriter encouraged in ways a computer could not. Since Derrick hadn't provided him with any correction fluid, there was no way to fix mistakes. Without the red computer underline, Bob wasn't even sure if he was correctly spelling every word. All he could do was concentrate on plot. And why use a single word when four would do? This was freewriting on steroids.

Absently, Bob reached for an apple and took a big bite. The first day he'd been ferociously hungry, but after a few days without easy access to junk food, clocks, or any reminders of the real world, the hunger had receded. Now he kept having to hitch up his sweatpants. Maybe all the walking had stretched them out.

He put his fingers back on the keys.

As Rowan rode away on his new horse, carrying the plunder plucked from the bodies of his foes, he remembered all the burning suns and starry nights he had seen. Was it all going to end here, on sands shifting faster than those in an hourglass?

DERRICK

Out of Game

R ickard ran through the woods, his crossed swords bouncing on his back. This was no longer Camp Tomawaka, a campground with a vaguely Native American–sounding name. And he was no longer Derrick Lavinsky, a teenage boy mostly invisible to the world.

Here in the mythical land of Cascadia, he was Rickard Starsworn, leader of the peasant rebellion. Despite having a price on his head and nothing in his belly, he would not be swayed from his mission to procure the Sacred Feather. Whoever possessed it could call down the army of gryphons from the sky.

Cascadia was a world full of magic and betrayal. Of brave fighters, cutthroat rogues, and majestic nobility. One thing it was not—definitely *not*—was the world of Swords and Shadows. While Derrick's dad had begun the LARP as a frank homage, over the years, dozens of new plot twists and characters had been introduced. And after the intellectual property lawsuit nine years ago, all overlapping names had been changed. So the game was now called Mysts of Cascadia and featured gryphons instead of unicorns.

If new players remarked on any remaining similarities, they were reminded to stay in character. If they continued to do so OOG (out of game), everyone knew to deny, deny, deny, just in case R. M. Haldon's publisher's lawyers had once again hired spies.

Even though Derrick's character, Rowan, had been renamed Rickard, the general outlines of the backstory remained the same. Derrick had reread the books many times in an effort to understand his character. It was *Mountains of the Moon* that had revealed Rowan for the hero—or perhaps antihero—he had been all along.

As Rickard drew closer to the clearing where he would meet Black Fox, the thief who'd promised to sell him the Sacred Feather, he slowed his pace, slipping from shadow to shadow.

Suddenly a woman shouted behind him. "I call forth a Web Spell." The spell (represented by a small beanbag filled with birdseed) slapped between his shoulder blades.

"By Ferdinand's Beard!" Rickard swore. He was currently without a Resist Spell to counteract the Web Spell. Now his arms and legs couldn't move.

Lady Katarina appeared in his peripheral vision, then moved to stand in front of him. Her long brown plaits were wound in a coronet around her head. Her smile was cold. Her left hand was hidden under her black fur cloak.

"Well met, Rickard. Why dost thou run through my forest without my leave? Mayhap you were looking for this?" She revealed what she had hidden under her cloak. The Sacred Feather of the Gryphons.

More players allied with Lady Katarina stepped

from behind trees and bushes, surrounding him. Most faces were familiar. A few not. Clearly, he'd been double-crossed by Black Fox.

"What kind of a man carries two swords and no shield?" a woman said mockingly. She hoisted her own shield and menacingly waved her sword.

"The kind of man who falsely fancies himself a fighter," her compatriot sneered. "And here he is, stuck without even unsheathing a weapon."

"He's not real smart, is he?" a third man said, shattering the illusion they were all working so hard to build. Derrick had never seen him before. He wasn't an NPC (non-player character), because they were provided with good-quality costumes. This guy's tunic was just a T-shirt turned inside out, with the hems cut off, and slit halfway down the center. The resulting V had been laced with one of the cut-off pieces of fabric. It was basically the cheapest, fastest costume you could make. He was wearing it over black sweatpants. Around his wrist, he'd tied another piece of fabric, but it did little to disguise that underneath it was a Fitbit. And on his feet were tennis shoes. Tennis shoes! What had the logistics committee been thinking when they checked this guy in? Had they been too busy pretending the apple juice in the tavern was really liquor?

The advent of the *Swords and Shadows* TV show had raised everyone's expectation of what proper garb should look like. It had also resulted in a plethora of Halloween costumes that weren't half bad, if you didn't mind polyester fur and plastic instead of metal. Halloween had only been two days ago. Yesterday, November 1, was also known as LARPers' Christmas, because costumes went on clearance. So this new player character had no justification for his sorry excuse for garb.

In contrast, Rickard was clad in black wool hose topped by a long-sleeved black tunic. Over that was a sleeveless dark green surcoat. Topping them all was a ruby red mantle fastened at the shoulder with an ornate brooch. After watching tons of YouTube videos, he'd painstakingly sewn the tunic, surcoat, and mantle, and designed the sigil on the mantle. The brooch had been a lucky find at Goodwill. On his feet were black leather slouch boots in a large ladies' size he'd picked up on sale last summer. Since he had no pockets (they weren't period), Rickard carried his belongings in a leather pouch slung over the belt around his surcoat.

Now he felt probing fingers. They belonged to the new guy. Physically putting your hands all over a captive was another lawsuit waiting to happen.

One of the other players cleared his throat. "Beg pardon, Blackheart Doombringer, but thou shouldst say, 'I search you,' and then Rickard shall yield his items."

Rickard bit back another groan at the new player's name. The Noun-Verbers (who gave themselves last names like Giantkiller, Dreamseeker, and Shadowwalker) were always the worst. But Blackheart Doombringer? Way to telegraph what kind of character you were playing!

Blackheart reluctantly withdrew his hands. "I thought he was paralyzed by that Web thingy."

Lady Katarina sighed. "Nay, not for a search."

Rickard welcomed the distracting discussion about

the rules. Because he knew something the others did not. He'd not come alone to this forest.

With a cry, five people charged from the trees on the other side of the clearing. Well, three people, an elf, and an ogre. Tonight they had all joined Rickard in his quest. An epic battle began to rage around him.

Someone freed Rickard with a Dispel Spell. He reached back, drew his two swords, and threw himself into battle. Each time he swung, he yelled, "Two!" for the number of damage points a single blow from one of his swords would cause.

Blackheart was fighting off the ogre. While normally Rickard wouldn't gang up on a player, he made an exception for Blackheart. But once he joined the fight, the ogre grunted and chased after a fleeing Lady Katarina.

Rickard circled around Blackheart, who had only a dagger. Unless Blackheart possessed a special spell to increase its powers, a dagger could do just one point of damage.

Rickard feinted with his right hand and then swung with his left. "Two!" he shouted, lightly tapping Blackheart's shoulder. Even though his sword was basically just PVC pipe wrapped in foam, it was against the rules to use any force. Injuries playing Mysts of Cascadia were rare, mostly just sprained ankles from tripping in the woods.

Blackheart did not grunt. He did not take a step back. He did not act as if anything had happened. He just rushed forward, swinging his dagger at Rickard's face, a forbidden target. He didn't even shout, "One."

Rickard easily evaded the blade, then whirled his left sword over his head and lightly tapped the same spot he had earlier. The sword in his right hand touched the matching spot on the other shoulder. "Two and two."

From the other man's sour expression, Rickard could tell he'd just used up all his points. According to the rules, Blackheart was now unconscious and bleeding out. Grumbling, he dropped to his knees but went no further. "Well, I guess I'm dead now."

"Then thou hadst better look it," Rickard said through gritted teeth, nudging him with the dull point of his sword.

BRIDGET

Stand on the Bones

"Leave us," King Tristan said to his guards.

"But my lord—" one began.

"Never question me. Is that understood?" His voice was quiet and all the more dangerous for that.

"Yes, sire."

He did not speak to Margarit until the guards' footsteps had faded away. "The people want to see red running down the headsman's axe. Even now there are peasants sleeping next to the stone so that they can feel your blood freckle their skin."

Bridget paused. For the past week, she'd been reading *King of Swords* aloud to Ajay at lunch. A fast talker, she'd already gotten through a big chunk of it. "Just a sec." She took a bite of the roti—a type of flatbread—that was part of his contribution to their unspoken trade of food for words. For a moment, she stilled her bouncing knees (sitting outside, she was always chilled, but it was a small price for spending time with Ajay) while she scribbled down the page number and *Is blood lucky?* in her notebook.

With each passing day, the weather had gotten colder and the outdoor tables less populated. Today it was in the low forties. The only other people outside were a couple in the far corner, wrapped in each other's arms.

Bridget and Ajay were sitting side by side, their backs to the cafeteria. On Friday, Ajay had declared that seeing their classmates distracted him from the fictional world he was trying to enter.

Today's chapters, full of cruelty and betrayal, had been some of her mom's favorites.

Better the headsman's axe, Margarit thought, than the oubliette King Tristan favored for his worst enemies. The single way in or out was via an iron grille in the ceiling. Once you were inside, it was only wide enough to allow you to stand. Its name came from the French oublier, *meaning "to forget."*

The year before, Tristan had ordered his own nephew, accused of plotting to overthrow him, lowered into the oubliette. The poor boy had been forced to stand on the bones of those who came before him. His screams were whispered about throughout the kingdom. Death, when it finally came, had been a mercy.

"Brutal," Ajay muttered, then added, "What's the matter? You look sad. Sad and cold. The sad part's new." He nudged her thermos of pumpkin soup—he now brought thermoses for both of them—into her hand. A curl of steam rose from it. "Drink some of this."

She took a sip. "Oh, that's good. What's the secret ingredient this time?" With Ajay, there was always at least one.

"Fresh coconut and kalonji." When she looked confused, he added, "Sometimes they're called nigella seeds. Or black onion, even though they're not related, because they're black and taste like toasted onions."

Bridget smacked her lips thoughtfully. Now she could taste both, the sweet and savory notes.

As she took another sip, he said, "You didn't answer me. What were you thinking about when you stopped reading?"

Sighing, she tried to adjust her coat to cover more of her legs. "About my mom. This was one of her favorite scenes."

"How old were you when she passed away?"

"Twelve. Right before *End of Forever* came out. But sometimes I wonder—what if Bob had just split the book in two and put out the first part earlier? Maybe she would have made it a little longer." It was suddenly hard to swallow.

"Bridget." He covered her hand with his own, brown on top of her white. "I'm sure she lived as long as she could. For your sake, not a book's."

It was the first time he'd deliberately touched her. He lifted his hand, but the tingle lingered.

Still, if the book had come out when her mom was still alive, Bridget would have read as slowly as possible.

Thinking of her mother and of Ajay's touch, she began to read again.

King Tristan grabbed Margarit's chin in his hand. Instead of trying to wrench away, she regarded him steadily as she remembered the fateful

98

night that had changed both of their lives. That had given her Jancy.

As she read, Bridget snuck a sideways glance at Ajay. When he first suggested they sit next to each other, she'd wondered if he was hinting about wanting to be closer. With each lunch period, she'd become more aware of his body, just a couple of inches away. Whenever he shifted, some part of him would brush her. Each touch lasted less than a second, but she felt it for long moments after. The way the back of her hand now still felt the warmth of his.

He dipped his head until they were nose to nose. The cell was quiet except for their exhalations echoing off the damp stone walls. Both breathing too loud, too fast.

The king pulled his lips back as if preparing to bite her. Margarit thought it possible he really wanted to kiss her, as he had another lifetime ago. Maybe the truth was that it was a little of both.

The back of Bridget's neck got hot as she uttered the word *kiss.* Her mouth was saying the words, but the rest of her was aware of how close Ajay was.

But what King Tristan wanted she couldn't give him, even though it meant she would die. He wanted Jancy. He wanted to ensure the blind seer's prophecy never came true.

The word *prophecy* made her think of Bob. *Eyes of the Forest* was supposed to answer all the questions raised by the previous books. But he was even more behind schedule than he'd been with *Mountains of the Moon.*

She had a fleeting memory of Derrick cornering her to talk about how eager he was for the final book. There were thousands of Derricks out there. Maybe millions. All that pressure must sometimes feel like an unbearable weight to Bob.

It had been a couple of weeks since she'd heard from him, the longest gap in the years they had been working together. A few days ago, she'd sent him a list of new words, terms, and ideas she'd added to the database. She had expected a reply, if not right away, then in a day or so. But none had come.

And now it occurred to her to wonder—should she be concerned? Even at twelve, she'd noticed Bob's plumpness, heard how he grunted whenever he went from standing to sitting and back again. The intervening years had not improved things.

Could something be wrong with Bob?

DERRICK

Mud and Moon

Yesterday Derrick had posted teasers from Bob's first amazing chapter on the dark web and then put the full chapter for sale. Afterward, he had sprinkled hints on Reddit, suggesting that the passages came from a copy leaked during the publishing process. Now as he sat in physics class, Derrick couldn't stop wondering how many had sold. For once, the sight of Bridget was not enough to distract him. Not even watching her and Ajay walk out together after the bell rang could divert his thoughts. He had bigger things to pay attention to.

At lunch Derrick checked the video feed of Bob, as he had between morning classes. The camera, powered by a rechargeable battery and running on cellular service, showed Bob typing away.

Derrick resisted the urge to visit his Bitcoin account. He would wait until it had been twenty-four hours. That way the amount would be even more impressive than if he had watched it come in one sale at a time. Plus he needed to give the whole thing time to gain traction. Once it did, he would post the second chapter, which was even more action-packed than the first. The screenshots were ready to be uploaded, but the timing had to be right. Too soon, and the desire wouldn't have a chance to build to a fever pitch. Too late, and it was possible it might have peaked.

Although *Eyes of the Forest* promised to be Bob's best book yet.

His mom had basically washed her hands of Bob, putting Derrick in charge of his day-to-day care and feeding. Claiming that any change in her schedule might arouse suspicion, Joanne still went to Bob's house every day. Only now instead of cleaning and cooking, her time was mostly spent watching Netflix and scrolling through Instagram.

The drive to the cabin dragged by. When Derrick finally arrived and walked into the bedroom, Bob was plunking away, with a satisfyingly thick stack of pages next to the typewriter. When he realized Derrick was in the room, Bob's shoulders jumped, but he didn't turn off the treadmill.

"Back from school already?" he asked without turning his head.

"It's after four." The room was half in shadow. "I'll heat up something for dinner soon."

"Okay," Bob said absently, already resuming typing as Derrick went back to the living room.

When Derrick sat on the couch, a broken spring poked through the worn cushion, but he barely felt it. What did it matter that the couch was falling apart? Soon they could afford to get a new one. Get a new everything. New cars, new TVs, new clothes, even a new house. He would no longer have to sew his own garb and make his own weapons.

He still had about twenty minutes to kill before the twenty-four hours were up. He checked Bob's email box, which had already lost its appeal. As usual, about half was spam. The remainder was people wanting to sell Bob more stuff to clutter up his office. Today it was dice made of real bones, a ship in a bottle that was also a whiskey decanter, and a dragon hourglass filled with black sand.

There was also a list of terms from Bridget—words, terms, and concepts she had added to the Swords and Shadows database. Just looking at her email address gave him a secret thrill. He stroked his thumb across it.

Aside from Bridget, the only other person who had written Bob was his agent. He had sent a bulleted list of new deals he had made for him. Countries so tiny Derrick had only a vague idea where they were, and for amounts that wouldn't even buy a decent latex sword.

Derrick checked the time on the top of his phone again. There. Exactly twenty-four hours. His trembling fingers made it hard to type the password into the Bitcoin account.

But when he finally opened it, the balance was zero. Zero. Had they been hacked? But there were no records of transactions out—or in—since he'd last sold some of Bob's ephemera. Which made no sense. People should be tripping over themselves. There were so many other Derricks out there. Fans who had either read the books from the beginning or heard about them early on through word of mouth or come to them later when the word of mouth became a roar. And since the TV show, even more had fallen down the rabbit hole. Realized Swords and Shadows was a much better place to spend your time than the real world.

The sample on the dark web did not allow for comments. But that didn't mean people didn't have them, as Derrick discovered when he clicked on Reddit's Swords and Shadows thread to gather clues as to what was happening.

People were clearly interested. The reaction to the excerpt from Bob's first chapter had been swift. And withering. Dozens of people, maybe even a hundred, had read the sample paragraphs Derrick had posted, the words that had thrilled him to the marrow, and then come back to Reddit to leave dismissive comments.

What was that crap?

I wouldn't let anyone PAY me to read that.

Talk about purple prose!

It reads like a bad mashup of every Swords and Shadows cliche.

R. M. Haldon wouldn't touch that with a ten-foot pole.

What did they do—hire someone on Craigslist or Fiverr?

That's simply bad fan fiction.

Was that a joke?

The more Derrick read, the angrier he got. What Bob had written was good. Better than good. Derrick was sure of it.

The phone rang, startling him. His mom. *Mud and moon*, Derrick swore to himself. "Hi, Mom!" He tried to add a lilt to his voice. If she didn't know what was going on, he wasn't going to tell her.

That hope was dashed a second later. "I just checked the account. Why is there no money in it?"

"These things probably take more time than a pair of socks."

"Where are all those so-called fans of yours? No one is buying. I don't understand. People were willing to pay a hundred for a piece of used dental floss, but they won't buy the book everyone's been asking for?"

Derrick had reached his own conclusions. "Yeah, but those things were different. We had pictures of him using the items. People seem worried that this is just fan fiction." And it was true there was a lot of bad fan fiction out there. Half of what went on at Mysts of Cascadia was basically bad fanfic.

The people who were looking and not buying must be viewing everything through the lens of suspicion. It was like those writers who tried releasing works under a pen name and found the reviews far less rapturous, at least until the true author was revealed.

If he could just prove to people that Bob was the one really doing the writing, then he was sure they *would* love it.

And suddenly Derrick got an idea. It was wonderful and awful at the same time.

The Haldon Cam.

All Derrick had to do was upload the footage of Bob typing away on his typewriter. That way would-be buyers would know it was real.

And then it would sell like hotcakes.

BRIDGET

My Daughter Will Have

G ood morning!"
        Her dad's voice startled Bridget. She snapped the laptop closed. She hadn't heard him get up—or come home in the first place. The only reason she'd known he was home was the suitcase sitting next to the front door.

Now he stood behind the recliner, yawning. He was wearing boxers and a white T-shirt.

How long had he been standing there? Long enough to see that Bridget hadn't been answering emails, doing homework, or working on the database? Long enough to see that she'd been writing?

"What time did you get in last night?" she asked. "I didn't even hear you."

Her dad flew home every Friday night, but by the time he landed and took a Lyft home, it was often after midnight. And less than forty-eight hours from now, in the darkness of what barely qualified as Monday morning, he would get up and take a Lyft back to the airport. During the week, he traveled all over the US selling food-grade plastics for Portland Plastic Pack, otherwise known as Triple P.

"Late. Our gate wasn't ready for some reason, and we just sat on the tarmac forever." He blew air through pursed lips. "It's just good to be home. Ready for some Marco's?"

"Sure." Breakfast on Saturday mornings at Marco's was a tradition that had started before her mom even got sick. Later this afternoon, they would play Scrabble, another family tradition.

"Let me just take a shower." He ran his hand through his salt-and-pepper hair, making it stand straight up. "I'll be ready in fifteen." He shambled back down the hall.

Once she heard the bathroom door close, Bridget opened up the laptop again. On it was—what exactly? It wasn't fan fiction, although it was set in a world where readers of Swords and Shadows would have felt at home. It featured a girl who was a little bit like Jancy. And a lot more like Bridget, at least the Bridget she would like to be. While this girl didn't have any magical powers, she did have courage, intelligence, and the ability to think on her feet. She managed to write a few more paragraphs before the shower stopped.

Bob had finally responded to her additions to the database with a brief thank-you. Usually he was more chatty—they could go back and forth on heraldry for hours—and she hoped it was a sign that he was finally working.

Thirty minutes later, Bridget and her Dad were seated at Marco's. The air was filled with the comforting smell of pancakes, fried potatoes, and coffee. Overhead, dozens of colorful umbrellas hung upside down from the ceiling, the way they had for as long as Bridget could remember. Now she wondered if anyone ever dusted inside them.

When the waitress came by, her dad said, "We'll both have coffee. And I'll have the chilaquiles. My daughter will have the breakfast skillet with cheddar and the eggs over easy, with whole wheat toast." Since that was what Bridget ordered every Saturday, he didn't even need to check in with her.

"Actually, I want to try something else," Bridget said, surprising herself, her dad, and even the waitress. She loved the breakfast skillet, which had potatoes, mushrooms, tomatoes, spinach, and lots and lots of garlic. Loved it so much that she never took the risk of trying anything else. What if it wasn't as good? What if she made the wrong choice?

But even though Ajay wasn't here, he'd somehow taken up residence in her head, pushing at her corners, encouraging her to try new things. "I think I'll have the pancakes with huckleberries and the huckleberry syrup."

"Okay, you heard the young lady," her dad said with a grin. "Pancakes with huckleberries, and make it a double." After the waitress left, he raised a quizzical eyebrow. "No breakfast skillet?"

"I've started eating lunch with this guy at school. Ajay Kapoor. He makes his own lunches and shares them with me. He cooks all this Indian food. Some of it's a little weird, but mostly it's amazing. It's made me think I should take more chances."

Her dad's smile was replaced with a more anxious expression. "Is this someone you're dating, Bridge?" When he'd started traveling more, he'd set down a long list of rules, including not having romantic partners over to the house. Which at the time had definitely been hypothetical.

The waitress set down their coffees, and Bridget took advantage of the pause to gather her thoughts. Even though they ate lunch together every day, Ajay still kept the same distance from her. Close enough to feel his warmth and far enough away that they weren't actually touching.

"No—he's just a friend, that's all." And she might have to accept that. "I've been reading Swords and Shadows to him at lunch. I've already finished *King of Swords*, and I just started *Darkest Heart*."

Her dad's expression morphed again. Bridget wasn't sure what it was exactly. It couldn't be disappointment, could it? "That sounds like the Bridget I know."

"Ajay brings his lunch in these cloth bags saturated with beeswax. If you warm them up with your hands, you can fold them."

His mouth twisted. "I've heard about those. But you can buy dozens of plastic bags for the price of just one of those beeswax bags. Maybe even thousands of plastic bags."

"That might be the point, Dad. Maybe people don't want to buy, use, and throw away thousands of plastic bags anymore."

He scrubbed his face with his hands. "Please, Bridget. I don't want to argue."

But they weren't arguing. Were they?

BOB

All That Crazy Stuff

The boy was finally, finally asleep in his room at the far end of the hall. Moving quietly so his shackles wouldn't jangle, Bob pulled the quilt off the bed and stuffed it into the crack under the door. With his foot tethered to the treadmill desk, he had to lean over and bear crawl to be able to finish snugging it into place.

Was it his imagination, or was there a little less gut getting in the way? His clothes seemed looser, but that could also be chalked up to the fact that he'd been wearing them for nearly two weeks. He'd only been allowed three showers since Derrick kidnapped him. The soles of his socks were beginning to wear through.

The first chapter he'd written for Derrick had been startling and fun. Bob had tried to keep the momentum going. Derrick's version of *Eyes of the Forest* was letting Bob release every wild thought, to vomit it all out on the page, great splashes of purple prose, padded to the point of absurdity. In the most recent section Bob had written today, he had given Rowan a lover, albeit one bought and paid for:

> *A crystalline sparkle in her eyes, the flame-haired slender harlot let a smile steal across her*

face as she regarded her rugged paramour, now
fast asleep. She knew not his name, and she guessed
the coin he had paid her with had been stolen. Yet
something about him inspired her to ponder leaving
behind this house of ill repute and throwing her lot
in with his.

Bob had a feeling the unnamed prostitute might not last long. And that her loss would scar Rowan.

Derrick would love the pages, but Bob could see it was all going a bit cliché. Familiar trope after familiar trope, strung together. The whore with a heart of gold. The beautiful girl who was not long for this world, who existed solely for the hero to sorrow over and then vow to revenge. In the TV show, the actress playing her would be expected to bare her breasts.

But women could be more than Madonnas or whores or old ladies. They had their own agency. Lilly had taught him that. And so much else. He absently stroked the scarf around his neck. The last time he'd been allowed a shower, he had washed it and then put it back on wet.

And while it was still great fun to write for Derrick, like a wild party, eventually you got tired of waking up on the living room floor with one of your shoes missing.

To prove Bob really was the one who had written the first chapter, Derrick had started broadcasting what he called the Haldon Cam on the dark web. It was like Animal Planet's Kitten Cam. Derrick's idea was Bob's fans would love to watch him typing away on his treadmill. Or as Derrick put it, "Watch his next bestseller being written in real time!" At night, he ran a loop of the day's footage of Bob typing away, thinking he was giving him time to sleep. In reality, Bob waited until Derrick was asleep and then started in on his other, secret project.

Bob was now writing two *Eyes of the Forest*, not one. One during the day, in full view of the Haldon Cam, and one secretly at night. One for Derrick and one for himself, like a parent making sure to divide things equally between two kids. Only in this case, one kid had no idea about the other.

For the past few days, he'd obediently climbed under the covers as soon as Derrick turned off the light. But he didn't sleep. Instead, he waited impatiently until the cabin was silent. Then he got back on the treadmill and wrote.

Now, working mostly by feel, Bob rolled a crisp new piece of paper into the typewriter. A faint, milky light reflected into the room from the snow, but it was enough. By now he was touch typing with ease. In some ways, it felt better to type in the dark when he couldn't even see what he wrote. No temptation to ball up the page the way he used to.

This second version of *Eyes of the Forest* was more measured. Tighter. Not that it lacked for twists and turns, but they weren't telegraphed. The sober version also made a hell of a lot more sense than Derrick's stream-of-conscious version. The new chapters were hidden in short stacks under the treadmill.

There were two of everything now. Two Jancys, two Rowans, two Prince Orwens. They overlapped and intertwined of course. But he was damned if he was going to give this kid his best stuff. Derrick seemed perfectly happy with the pages Bob just dashed off without too much thought.

And letting all that crazy stuff loose was making something flower in Bob. He was doing the best writing he ever had.

Twice over.

DERRICK

Keep It in Character

Saturday night, and the Jolly Pirate tavern in Cascadia was packed. Guilds were holding meetings, elves were celebrating a name day, and adventuring groups were rehashing that day's battles.

Rickard pulled the door closed behind him. The room was lit with candle holders and lanterns—both powered by LED bulbs. Period authenticity took a back seat to the fire marshal.

Crowding the long benches along the tables were lords and ladies, commoners and craftsmen, spies and soldiers, and the occasional elf or ogre. They were dicing, playing cards, or exchanging in-game gold for treats like bread or pie that been prepared OOG and then brought here. Some wore handmade costumes that looked it while others' garb featured real ermine or hand-forged chain mail. The young man standing just inside the door felt his point of view begin to shift from Rickard's to Derrick's. In real life the players were college students, Uber drivers, exterminators, and architects. They worked at banks and call centers. More than one was a veteran with PTSD who said LARPing helped them deal.

It was time to spread the word about the once-in-a-lifetime chance to read R. M. Haldon's new book. Since Derrick had started streaming the Haldon Cam, the first chapter alone had already sold over a hundred copies, and most buyers had come back for chapters two and three. The feedback on Reddit had completely turned around.

Derrick had already ordered custom-made armor from Austria for a price that would have bought a good used car, but it wouldn't be ready for another month. Tonight the only evidence of his newfound wealth was the new scarlet-lined black cloak he'd bought on Etsy.

Everyone was drinking. Some players were tavern jockeys who would spend most of their weekend here. But just like the candles had been replaced with their LED counterparts, the spirits were actually juice. As the night wore on, a few players would still pretend to be drunk. Sometimes hookups were blamed on too much mead.

Derrick felt a cold wind as the door opened again. A shout went up from the tables. It was Crispin, also known as Rickard's father. OOG, Crispin was Curtis and still Derrick's dad. His father had had custody on every LARP weekend. Derrick had been playing alongside him since he was eight, in one of the limited roles children were allowed to take. Since turning sixteen, Derrick had been able to be a full-fledged PC, moving quickly up the ranks thanks to all his IG knowledge. And it didn't hurt that the character Rickard was based on had gained more importance with each book.

On weekdays Curtis was an accountant, but in Cascadia, Crispin was a silver-tongued rogue working both ends against the middle. He was tall, like Derrick, but more muscular. Even though Derrick thought they looked alike, new players always seemed surprised to find out they were real-life father and son.

"What ho, friends!" Crispin cried. He was grinning, his arms around Lady Katarina and a stone elf named Sheena. As Cascadia's founder, he drew women like flowers drew bees.

He clapped one hand on Derrick's shoulder as he made his way to the center of the crowd. Derrick felt a familiar tangle of jealousy and love. But then he remembered. The coins in his father's purse had no value OOG. But the money Derrick was making from selling Bob's work could be spent anyplace.

Turning away, he pushed himself deeper into the tavern. A small crowd was gathered around Nellique. In front of her were a number of wire tools. Sticking two in the lock of a small wooden box, she began to manipulate them, her tongue poking between her teeth. While Nellique had had to buy the legerdemain skill to become a locksmith, it didn't guarantee she would actually be able to get into the box. To open the lock, she had to pick it for real.

New people came to Cascadia expecting a game, but this was as close to real life as you could get. You didn't roll dice to see if you had the charisma necessary to pull a great con, or the dexterity to hide in the shadows, or the intelligence to figure out a secret code. You had to actually be able to do those things. If you wanted to strike an enemy with your arrow, then you had to physically throw your arrow representation and hit them with it.

As Derrick cast his eyes over the crowd, he heard an exaggerated evil laugh. Before he looked, he knew it belonged to Blackheart Doombringer. Inwardly Derrick groaned when he saw he was still wearing the same half-assed costume made from an inside-out T-shirt. What an idiot. With that laugh, he was just putting people on their guard. He should be portraying himself as a valiant man wanting to right the world's wrongs. In fact, the best bad guys probably considered themselves good ones.

It was clear Blackheart hoped to begin near the top of Cascadia's hierarchy. But that wasn't the way it worked. New players had to put time and effort into their costumes, always stay in character, and take their role-playing seriously. Those who did found it wasn't long until the old-timers noticed, hiring them for a quest or as bodyguards. With luck, tales of their adventures might someday be retold by storytellers over cups of spiced cider.

Putting aside his annoyance, Derrick zeroed in on Baltus, sitting alone in a back corner. In real life—not that Derrick thought Cascadia was any less real—Baltus was named Stan, and Stan was a lawyer who drove a brand-new BMW. Which meant he must own some serious coin OOG. And he was in his sixties, meaning he probably didn't spend much time on Reddit.

"What ho, Baltus?" Derrick called out.

"Come sit with me." Baltus patted the empty bench next to him.

After they exchanged their respective stories of that day's adventures, Derrick leaned nearer, conspiratorial. "Have you heard that the Great Storyteller is working on the next volume to his saga?" Great Storyteller was their name for R. M. Haldon. In game, out-of-game things were referred to by other names. Pens were quills. Cars were dragons. Phones were magic boxes. The internet was the mist market.

Stan waved a hand. "That's been bandied about since I was knee-high to a steed."

"Nay, 'tis true. And it is being sold segment by segment."

"What? You mean like online?"

A woman in a wimple turned her head at the forbidden word. "Keep it in character please," she murmured.

Derrick continued. "Not on the mist market, but its darker twin." How to put it? "The um, the shadowy mesh. For the coin of the realm which is known as a bit."

Baltus's forehead wrinkled. "You mean for Bit"— Derrick laid a hand on his arm, and he lowered his voice. "For Bitcoin on the dark web?" When Derrick nodded, the other man reared back. "Why wouldst the Maker do that?"

"Does he not need coin, the same as any man?" It wasn't even exactly a lie.

"Nay! You blaspheme! He is no mere mortal."

Derrick was unsure how much Stan was joking. Among the original players of Cascadia, R. M. Haldon was seen as something close to a god. What would Stan think if he could see Bob now, plodding along on a treadmill dressed in sagging sweats?

Derrick shrugged. "It has been too long since the Great Storyteller told a new story. People sate their urges with tales from other gods."

"What need has he to offer his stories on the shadowy mesh? Can he not just use the market square as he has always done?"

"These are more exclusive. And more"—Derrick rubbed his fingers together, the universal sign for expensive.

After looking around, Stan leaned forward and lowered his voice. "I would give a lot to read *Eyes of the Forest*."

"Then check the Red Thread." Red Thread was IG code for Reddit. "And follow the clues you find there."

"Excuse me, then," Stan said, getting to his feet. "I shall go to my dragon and check my magic box."

Derrick spent the next few hours dropping hints. And by the time he surreptitiously checked his own magic box in his dragon, another twelve buyers had purchased the first chapter.

BOB

Haldon Cam

Shoulders heaving, Bob bent over, braced his hands on his knees, and tried to catch his breath. It wasn't easy doing jumping jacks.

Not to mention when doing them was entirely someone else's idea.

"Okay," Joanne said from the doorway, out of reach of the camera. Today she was wearing a fur coat Bob thought was actually made of real fur from some poor unfortunate animals. He was no expert in women's fashion, but now that he was making good money for them, Joanne seemed intent on spending it. Every time he saw her, she had on some new, expensive-looking outfit. "The next one says, 'Do the funky chicken.'"

Derrick was off LARPing, so Joanne was the one minding Bob. He much preferred Derrick.

Bob groaned. "What is that even supposed to look like?" His sweatshirt was sticking to the small of his back.

Joanne exhaled impatiently. "I think you're supposed to squat and walk around with your thumbs tucked in your armpits, flapping your arms." She demonstrated with the arm that wasn't holding the stun gun. "You know. Like a chicken."

Bob didn't move.

For an incentive, Joanne pressed the button on the side of the stun gun, out of sight of the camera. A white bolt of current shot between the two poles with a *tat-tat-tat* that sounded like rapid fireworks.

He flinched. Derrick loved him for his writing. Joanne didn't love him for anything, not even for the money that had made her new fur coat possible.

"Hurry up. They're paying three hundred dollars."

A few days after the Haldon Cam went live, someone had offered money. Not to buy the first chapter, but to watch Bob do push-ups. Derrick had said no, but Joanne had overruled him. As far as Bob could tell, Joanne enjoyed the extra dollop of humiliation it added to his situation.

And once she forced Bob to do them, with some off-camera persuasion from the stun gun (Bob managed five before he had to switch to his knees), the floodgates opened. It turned out people would pay a lot to watch Bob (or someone who at least bore a strong resemblance to Bob) do a wide variety of things. Dance like John Travolta. (For that, he'd just pointed in various directions while swiveling his hips.) Play air guitar. Do the can-can.

Now Bob tucked his thumbs in his armpits, bent his knees, and shuffled around, flapping his elbows. It felt strange, and it wasn't just because he was pretending to be a chicken while being broadcast on some secret corner of the internet. It also felt strange because the spare tire around his middle was truly disappearing. Almost three weeks on the treadmill, and his new nearly carb-free diet was having an effect. He thought he was down at least ten pounds. The new sweats Joanne had brought Bob when she came to give Derrick a break were just an XL.

Bob's knees were protesting. Finally, he straightened to his full height. "That's enough. I can't do it anymore."

Joanne shrugged. "Okay. Let's see what the next one is."

"I'm not just talking about the chicken! I mean I'm not going to keep shaking my money maker or marching around like a German soldier. I'm not a marionette. I'm a person!" He pointed at the camera. "I'm not their dancing monkey!"

Whoever was watching this could not hear his complaints. Derrick kept the sound off in case Bob pleaded for help and someone listened.

"Oh wait, I think that's on the list." Joanne looked down at her phone.

To his horror, Bob realized she wasn't joking. "I'm supposed to be writing, Joanne. Don't you remember? This is just getting in the way of my finishing *Eyes of the Forest*."

Joanne shrugged. "Derrick's got several chapters in reserve. And right now, we're making nearly as much on this as we are on the chapters."

"Please, Joanne. Please let me go back to the book." Even the fake book was slowly starting to not be such a fake. Letting go of all his expectations was turning out to be perversely useful.

"First you have to sing 'Happy Birthday' to somebody

named Mabel. I'll turn on the sound for that. They want you to look right at the camera, and they want a lot of enthusiasm."

Exhaustion weighted his bones. "No. I'm not going to. That's enough."

Joanne grabbed his wrist and yanked him out of camera range. The next thing he felt was the stun gun against his neck.

Before she could press the button, he yelled, "Okay! Okay!"

"And look cheerful!" Joanne poised a thumb over her phone. "I'm turning on the sound, but if you say anything but the lyrics, I will stun you and I won't stop."

Stepping back into the camera's range, Bob pulled his lips up into a rictus grin. At least the song was mercifully short. "Happy birthday, dear Mabel. Happy birthday to you." His voice cracked as he finished the last line.

Joanne clicked the button on her phone to turn the sound off again. "Okay, just one more, Bob, and then you can write. I need you to pee like a dog."

His face went hot. "I'm not going to pee on camera!"

She shrugged. "Just lift your leg and pretend. And then I'll let you write until it's time to go to bed."

"I'm not doing it." Bob forced himself to confront the truth that had been nagging at him since he first woke up in this room. "I mean, let's be realistic. You two are never going to let me go, are you? As soon as the book is done, you'll kill me."

Joanne made a scoffing sound. "Oh, stop being so dramatic. Once the book is done, we'll let you go."

He made a raspberry noise. "Isn't that what every kidnapper says?"

"But you don't understand." Her grin was flat. "That day you met Derrick, he recorded you guys thinking up the whole plan. Who's going to listen to you once they realize you were a willing participant? What's happening now is exactly what you wanted. What you talked to me about endlessly." She moved her hand like a mouth flapping open and closed. "Blah, blah, I've got writer's block, blah, blah, I wish I could write. Do you know how sick I got of your whining? By the time this is over, you'll finally have the book done. Your publisher will be happy. Your fans will be happy, especially the ones who got it early. And you've even lost some weight. Frankly, all of us are already winning." She shrugged. "But if it means that much to you, Bob, then go ahead and write. And we'll do the other stuff later."

BRIDGET

I'm Doing This for You

Thwack! Thwack! Ignoring the tears in her eyes, Bridget brought down the knife again and again.

But the onion was winning this war.

Blinking, she tried to focus on the butter chicken recipe Ajay had written out for her. He'd scribbled notes in the margins, but it was still mostly a foreign language to her. Like what did "dice" mean, exactly? At least when she had cut the chicken breast into one-inch pieces, she'd known exactly how big that was. The pieces of chicken were now marinating in olive oil, lemon juice, and curry powder. Ajay roasted and ground his own individual spices, but he'd simplified the recipe for her. She hadn't even known that curry was a blend of spices.

Concentrating on cooking took Bridget's mind off wondering where her dad was. He'd promised to be home by the time she got back from school, which never happened. But when she'd unlocked the door an hour ago, the house had been as empty as ever.

He was probably caught at the airport. The day before Thanksgiving was always a zoo. Tomorrow they would go out to eat and then go to the multiplex and watch movie after movie, which had been the tradition ever since her mom died. Her dad would be home for four whole days.

Thanks to his job, Bridget knew there was no single substance called "plastic." Her cutting board was made from high-density polyethylene plastic (HDPE or number 2) as was the jug in the fridge holding skim milk. The bottles of Diet Coke and salad dressing that sat next to the milk were made from polyethylene terephthalate (PET or number 1), as were the plastic clamshells holding tomatoes on the counter. PET could stand up to acidic foods like pickles, but you could never wash away the smell once it stored food with strong odors.

The containers she'd put the leftovers in after dinner were polypropylene (PP or number 5), which could go from cupboard to fridge to microwave to dishwasher and back to cupboard without breaking, melting, or degrading. And polycarbonate (PC or number 7) was used to make reusable water bottles and baby bottles. At least it had been until people started worrying about one ingredient: bisphenol A (BPA).

Her dad sold low-density polyethylene (LDPE, or number 4). Pliable, it was perfect for squeeze bottles and plastic film that wrapped everything from frozen food to bread to meat.

Unfortunately, the chemicals that made plastic stable and flexible could leach into food. Her dad tried to reassure customers the FDA had strict regulations about how much. But people didn't always trust the government to look out for their best interests. And many, like Ajay, saw plastic as a not-very-necessary evil.

Bridget turned on the burner underneath the frying pan and added a tablespoon each of butter and olive oil as the recipe instructed. After the butter melted, she slid in the chopped onion. It landed with a sizzle. Next she used her fingernail to separate four cloves from a head of garlic. Following Ajay's directions, she hit them with the side of the knife to loosen the skin.

At the sound of her dad's voice, she jumped. She hadn't even heard him come in.

"What's all this?" With a grin that didn't disguise his exhaustion, he set down his suitcase and commuter backpack.

"I'm making dinner."

"By yourself?" He raised an eyebrow. "Is this from one of those meal kit companies?"

"Stop it!" Bridget shook the knife mock-threateningly. "It's from a real recipe for butter chicken that Ajay gave me. And I braved the Thanksgiving crowds at a real grocery store to buy the ingredients." As his expression changed, she added, "What's the matter?"

"Nothing." He looked away.

"Tell me."

"It's just the way you move your hands when you talk. You look so like your mom."

Bridget's memories of the time before her mother got sick were tattered and faded. But if she wanted to know what she would look like as an adult, all she had to do was check out the half-dozen framed photographs on the walls. Every year, she and her dad got older and further away from the people they'd been in those photos, while her mother stayed exactly the same. And every year, Bridget looked more like her. The same heart-shaped face. The same snub nose. The same milk-pale skin. The same russet hair that curled at the ends.

Her dad stepped into the kitchen. "Can I help?"

"Sure." She looked back down at the recipe. "Can you grate a couple of tablespoons of ginger?"

He gave the onions a stir and then peeled the knob of ginger. Bridget hadn't even known you needed to do that. She began mincing the garlic. "Mince" sounded smaller than "dice," so she chopped the cloves fine. The savory smell once she added them to the skillet made her mouth flood with water. Next to her, her dad grated shreds of ginger into the pan, making everything smell even better.

"Sorry I was late." He sighed. "My second flight was delayed, and then my phone ran out of battery. At least I had a chance to catch up on paperwork." He called it paperwork, even though it was all on his laptop. "I never dreamed I'd come back to real home cooking." When her dad traveled, he gravitated toward fast food, which was comforting, familiar, and cheap.

"I wanted to celebrate you being home on a weekday." She added a can of tomato puree, two more tablespoons of butter, and even more curry powder to the pan. "It feels like I don't ever see you anymore."

He stiffened. "Do you think I like it, Bridge? I get up in the morning alone, have breakfast alone, drive to my first call alone, go through more calls alone, eat lunch alone, make more calls and then drive back to my hotel at the end of the day. Alone."

Bridget stopped stirring. "What do you think my life is like, Dad? It's mostly like yours, minus the travel." Most of her friendships had fallen away during the years her mom was sick. After her mom died, her dad started working more hours. Once Bridget turned sixteen, he'd moved from inside sales to a job that kept him away from home for days at a time. Ajay was the first real friend Bridget had made in years.

And that's all he seemed to be—a friend. Which was fine.

He took a deep breath. "Look, Bridge, there's no easy way to say this. Triple P is sending me down to South America for a month. I'm flying out Sunday, and I won't be back until Christmas Eve."

"What?" It felt like the floor was falling from under her feet. "Are you serious, Dad?" The weekdays always felt so lonely. Sometimes she left the TV on just to hear other people's voices.

"If you weren't you, I would have said no." He leaned against the refrigerator. "There's not a lot of teens you could leave that long by themselves. But you've got a good head on your shoulders. And this is a chance to get my numbers up."

He was always chasing after a better sales number. Triple P gave him monthly, quarterly, and annual targets. In September, one of his biggest clients had declared bankruptcy and he'd missed his monthly target. Badly. That had thrown off his quarterly and annual targets. Now he was running just to stay in place.

"But South America?" She kept her eyes on the pan

as she added the chicken. If she looked at him, she would start crying. "Why do you have to go so far away?"

"There's no growth left in the domestic market. Down there, they're more open to plastics. Here, people think plastic is evil. They don't care that it doesn't break or corrode, or that it keeps out microorganisms, or helps food stay fresh and tasty. Now customers say they want unbleached paper, or something recyclable or at least compostable. And all these ecofriendly, save-the-planet companies are out there selling reusable containers, or glass or ceramics or that beeswax stuff your friend uses." He made a raspberry sound. "They're expensive and impractical."

"Everyone can see the climate is changing," she said, giving the pan a stir. "People my age worry the world's all messed up and it's too late to fix it. And now, even if it has numbers stamped on the bottom, they say most plastic isn't recyclable."

"The truth is, it probably never was recycled." He shook his head. "And whose fault is that? Americans are terrible sorters. People were just throwing everything in the recycling bin and feeling virtuous. They thought someone on the other end knew all the rules and would figure it out for them. That's why no country wants to take our plastic anymore, because most of it is really garbage."

Bridget ran hot water and then filled the measuring cup to the amount Ajay had written down to make the basmati rice. "So you're just going to leave me here all by myself and go down to sell plastic to poor countries that definitely won't recycle it?"

He ran a hand down his face. "Look, Bridget, what do

you want me to do? This is what I know. Do you think I want to be away from you? But I need to if I want to keep my job. And selling plastic beats not having a job at all."

"What do you mean?" She put the pot on the burner, turned it on, and salted the water. "Are you worried about being fired?"

To her shock, he nodded.

"But you work so hard! That can't be legal."

"It doesn't matter how hard I work if I don't make my numbers. Sure, Triple P can't fire me for being a man, or white, or a lapsed Lutheran. But firing me for not making my sales numbers? That's totally legal."

"It's not fair!"

"Legal and fair can be different things." He leaned against the counter. "Don't you understand, Bridget? I have to do this for you. For us."

AJAY

Sudden Turns of Fate

A jay woke up when his mom and sister came home at six A.M. He pulled the pillow over his head, but it didn't cover the sounds of their chatter and laughter as they exclaimed over their finds. Crazy people got up at four A.M. on Black Friday to save money. Indians got up at one A.M. on Black Friday and laughed smugly when the four A.M. crowd arrived and were forced to stand behind them in line and then pick through their shopping leftovers.

Yesterday Ajay had gone all out, cooked a meal that interpreted a traditional Thanksgiving meal though an Indian lens. Herbed paneer, the cheese squeaky and fresh. Cumin roasted carrots. Scalloped potatoes made with masala and coconut milk. Before roasting the turkey, he'd marinated it overnight in freshly toasted spices and homemade yogurt. On the side, he had served tangy chutney and, to cool everything off, a bowl of raita made with more yogurt, chopped cucumber, and spices.

The yogurt he'd used was a direct descendant of the yogurt his dead grandmother had brought to the US forty years earlier. She'd wrapped a tiny container of it in carbon paper, believing that an airport X-ray machine couldn't detect it. One of her first acts in America had been to use that bit of yogurt to start a new batch. And week after week, year after year, the cycle continued, the old giving birth to the new. The fridge always held yogurt, and it was eaten with every meal, offering a cooling respite to spices, a tang to soups, a lift to desserts. As usual, his grandfather, his dead grandmother's widower, had gotten a little teary-eyed when he tasted the telltale tang of the raita. The meal had been another unqualified success.

Now the Thanksgiving leftovers were refrigerated in the collection of old pickle, chutney, and jaggery powder containers that his frugal parents used instead of Tupperware.

Ajay sighed in frustration. The chatter in the living room was not abating. It was clear he was not going to be able to go to sleep, even though the sun had not yet started to rise. Yesterday, he had had family and food to distract him. But today he was fully aware of Bridget's absence. He wouldn't be with her for three more long days. He missed seeing her blow on her cold fingers, hearing the humming sound she made when she tasted a dish he'd made. Watching her lips as she read aloud.

And now to his surprise, Ajay found he also missed the world of Swords and Shadows. The twists, the secrets, the betrayals, the doomed loves, the sudden turns of fate. On Wednesday, Bridget had finished reading *Unicorn Wars*, the third book in the series. The book had actually ended with two of the main characters on the gallows, nooses around their necks. Bridget had refused to tell him, but Ajay was pretty sure they would live. At least he hoped so. On Monday she would start *Court of Sorrows* and he would know for sure. But the idea of having to wait that long now seemed untenable.

Trying to distract himself, he picked up his phone. And then somehow he found himself clicking on Multnomah County Library's website. The print and ebook editions for *Court of Sorrows* weren't available. But the audiobook was. And before Ajay could think twice, he clicked on the link to download it.

DERRICK

Much Better

All through physics class, Derrick kept his eyes on Bridget, as he always did. But he hadn't spoken to her since two days after he'd taken Bob.

At least, not that Bridget knew of. In reality, it had been his fingers writing Bob's emails in response to her latest additions to the database. First, Derrick had gone back through Bob's outbox to see how he'd phrased them in the past. Most were brusque, a few chatty. As Bob, Derrick had replied to the first email of Bridget's that he'd seen with a quick "Thanks!" After her second submission, he had risked a few sentences complimenting her on her thoroughness. And blushed at her smiling emoticon in reply.

Today, Bridget's flame-red hair was tucked behind the pale shells of her ears. Ever since being caught by Mr. Manning, she had stopped surreptitiously listening to Swords and Shadows. While Derrick loved the stories, Bridget must practically inhabit them. Someday he hoped to introduce her to Cascadia. She would discover there were even better things than books. In Cascadia, you could be the hero of the story. And who didn't want that?

Class broke for lunch. Derrick sat at the same table he shared with the other quiet kids, but now he always made sure to face the window. This way he could watch Bridget and Ajay as if they were on a giant muted TV. As the days had passed, Derrick's jealousy had abated. The closest Ajay came to touching Bridget was when he handed her something to eat. Maybe he didn't even like girls.

But it was clear he was falling for the world of Swords and Shadows. While Bridget read, Ajay turned his face toward her like a flower toward the sun, his expressions ranging from fear to sadness. If anything, Derrick told himself, that was what he was jealous of. Not Bridget's attention, but being able to hear the books fresh. While the parts of *Eyes of the Forest* he'd read so far were amazing, it was still set in a world he already knew well.

After school ended, he drove home instead of to the cabin. This weekend, his mom would be in charge of Bob while Derrick was off in Cascadia.

Derrick had felt oddly empty lately, even though he was finally getting to read *Eyes of the Forest*. It must be the lack of LARP. Holidays messed up the whole schedule, plus they met less frequently during the winter months. The prospect of having to do battle in the middle of a downpour or sleep in an unheated cabin tended to cut down on the number of participants.

When he got home, the porch was piled high with boxes. Mostly from UPS, but there were two from Amazon, and one each from FedEx and DHL. The majority were for his mom, but not the five boxes that had been shipped from Austria. His custom gear was finally here!

He pushed all the boxes inside the door, closed it, then grabbed the black drawstring bag holding his garb from his room. After hurrying into his black wool hose and long-sleeved tunic, he opened the first box. Black knee-length boots that laced up the back and cuffed at the top. He stroked the soft, supple leather as he pulled them over his hose, then took a few steps. It was like walking on a cloud. They definitely wouldn't pinch his toes. Derrick looked closer. The contrast between the new leather and his old hose was striking. He had never noticed, but the wool was faded, more charcoal than midnight.

The next box held a black padded gambeson, which was basically a coat that fastened with leather straps and buckles. He slipped into it, relieved at how well it fit. While Middle Ages clothing wasn't particularly form-fitting and he had emailed his measurements, part of Derrick had worried that his translation from inches to centimeters was off.

The remaining three boxes held his new armor. Even in the weak winter sunlight, the pieces shone like mirrors. Silver jointed-metal leg guards. A breastplate topped with a semicircular gorget to protect the upper chest. Jointed arm guards that ended in articulated metal gloves. And finally spaulders that covered his shoulders and connected with the arm guards.

When people asked, Derrick's plan was to say that some pissed-off girl on eBay was selling her ex-boyfriend's gear and didn't realize what she had.

He snapped all the pieces into place, topped them

with his new scarlet-lined black cloak, and clanked down the hall to the bathroom with its full-length mirror.

When Derrick looked at his reflection, his eyes regarded him from a stranger's face. He wouldn't have been out of place in a movie. Not as an extra either, but as the lead. He was wearing everything he'd dreamed of for years. Pieces he'd bookmarked on websites or regarded enviously when they graced some doughy trauma surgeon. But now they were all his.

So why did it all feel so flat, like he was miming joy instead of really feeling it?

And then Derrick realized what was missing. He had ordered a top-of-the-line latex sword and dagger, but they hadn't yet been delivered. The quality was supposed to be so good that you could hold them inches from your eyes and still think they were metal.

Without weapons, of course he couldn't get the full effect.

Derrick didn't know his mom had come home until she appeared out in the hall, her eyes narrowed and her arms full of shopping bags. They regarded each other in silence, each of them silently daring the other to comment on their spending. Finally, she shrugged and continued on to her bedroom. Derrick retrieved his street clothes and duffel from the living room and then changed back into them, carefully nesting his new gear so that it all fit into his bag.

When he came out, his mom was gathering up things to take to the cabin. He handed over the keys.

"Where's the stun gun?" she asked.

"I left it at the cabin." He swallowed. "You're not going to hurt him, are you?"

She busied herself with her bags. "We've gotten a lot of requests for the Haldon Cam."

"Mom—that's not what's important. We did this so Bob would write. Not so he could be humiliated online."

"The money's good. Aren't you the one taking economics? I'm sure we make more per minute with Bob on cam than we do on him writing."

It felt like the more his mom had, the more she wanted. Although was Derrick much better? If they had had a different kind of relationship, he might have asked her if all this new stuff left her feeling as empty as he did.

"If your only focus is the money, then why aren't you cleaning out his checking account?"

"Because that would be way more out in the open and the bank might notice. People might start asking questions."

Her words set off an uncomfortable echo. Eventually Bob would finish the book, and they would let him go. People might start asking questions then.

And would Bob be willing to go along?

BOB

A Thousand and One Nights

The door to Bob's room opened. He didn't turn, but he could feel Joanne's glare, hot on the back of his neck, as he kept walking to nowhere. After hundreds of miles on the treadmill, his feet had toughened as his body slimmed down. This weekend, Derrick was off LARPing, leaving Bob to the not-so-tender mercies of his mother.

In no hurry to interact with her, Bob kept typing. Or writing. Or whatever it was he was doing with the book he was parceling out to Derrick.

Bob was nearly done with both books. This one for Derrick and the other, hidden underneath his feet, that he was writing for himself.

"Down on your knees, yokel, and pay proper homage to your sovereign ruler," King Orwen ordered Rowan, sitting on his jeweled throne in pasty splendor.

Rowan remained standing, head held high, dressed in tattered rags.

A hush fell over the hall as people awaited the king's capricious wrath.

At Rowan's insolence, King Orwen curled his
soft hands into fists. "I am your new sovereign ruler.
You must kneel."

But Rowan didn't move a single firm muscle. At
a nod from the king, the soldier standing to Rowan's
left smote him in the face with the flat of his sword.
The blow knocked his battered helmet to the marble
floor with an echoing clang.

Even though Rowan staggered, he remained on
his feet, blood trickling from his ear.

"Kneel before me and tremble, you piteous
wretch, or I—"

A newly bejeweled hand reached past Bob to hit the
red button on the treadmill's control panel. "Okay, it's
time to stop. It's well past time."

The treadmill coasted to a halt as he turned to face
Joanne, tugging up his too-loose pants over what used to
be his belly. She was holding a JCPenney bag as well as
the stun gun.

"I brought you some new sweats." Her nose wrinkled.
"Size L. I guess I'll sell the ones you're wearing now. Your
last set went for $376.11."

The new sweats were a hideous orange-yellow, the
color of an egg yolk, a color he could not imagine looking
good on anyone. Which was probably why Joanne had
chosen it.

It was clear that she herself wasn't shopping at
JCPenney, at least not any longer. Diamonds the size of
dimes tugged at her earlobes. Bob was no connoisseur
of fashion, but even he could tell that her high-collared

black jacket, matching slacks, and pointy high heels with red soles must be expensive.

"Thank you." He reached for the clothes.

She held the bag out of reach. "First, I have some viewer requests."

Bob let out a heavy sigh. He'd gotten used to everything—the healthy food, the treadmill, the hours of writing—except the tricks.

"Can't we just skip this part, Joanne? Derrick told me the chapters are selling well." Based on the hints the boy had dropped, Bob had done the math in his head. He'd already made them well over a hundred thousand dollars. "Don't you want me to write?"

She cocked her head. "Don't you mean that's what *you* want, Bob?"

He hesitated, sensing a trap.

"Let's just say I'm not that interested in what *you* want. My ex fell in love with your books to the point that he didn't care about real life. Didn't care about me. And now Derrick is following the same path. So if I can make some extra money humiliating you? It seems like I deserve that, at least."

For the next hour, Bob twerked, did Tai Chi, and pretended to play table tennis while Joanne watched from the doorway. The whole time, she regarded him like something she'd discovered on the bottom of one of her new shoes and was now desperate to scrape off.

That look made Bob face reality. Once he finished the book, he would lose all value to her. Even Derrick would no longer care about the person who had written all those words. Bob would be nothing but a liability. What incentive would they have to let him go?

So what if they had a video of him agreeing to their plans? It wasn't like the three of them had signed a legally binding contract. It had been a drunken conversation on his part, nothing more. What were the chances the video would hold up in court, especially once he testified that he'd begged to be released?

Finishing the book might just get him killed.

So obviously Bob couldn't finish. Instead, he might need to be like Scheherazade in *A Thousand and One Nights*. In that ancient tale, when an Arabian king found out his first wife had been unfaithful to him, he put her to death. He decided that he would start each day by beheading the previous day's wife and then marrying a new young woman. That way, she wouldn't have the opportunity to cheat.

But when Scheherazade became the new wife, she spent the night telling an exciting tale. As dawn broke, she stopped in the middle. The king spared her life for another day. The following night, Scheherazade finished the story and then began a second, even more thrilling story. At dawn, she again stopped halfway through. Again, the king spared her life for one more day so she could finish.

And so the king kept Scheherazade alive day by day.

In the fable, at the end of a thousand and one nights and a thousand stories, Scheherazade told the king that she had no more tales. But during those nights, the king had fallen in love with her. He spared her life and made her his queen.

Bob had always found the ending a touch questionable. Who would want to marry a man who had killed dozens of other women before you?

But maybe Scheherazade had just been making the best of a bad situation, the way Bob was going to have to.

BOB

Time to Call a Halt

Since realizing his life depended on never finishing *Eyes of the Forest*, Bob had added two fresh characters and a whole new subplot to Derrick's version of the book. But the more he thought about it, the more he knew that he was only stalling the inevitable. Eventually, somebody was going to tire of things. Readers. Derrick. Joanne. Or maybe all three.

When Derrick carried in his Lean Cuisine dinner, steaming in the chilly room, Bob set into motion the new, desperate plan he had come up with.

"Look, Derrick, the closer I get to the end of the book, the more I realize I need my researcher. Bridget keeps track of all the details." His rueful smile wasn't entirely fake. "Over the years, I've just created too much. Too many creatures, too many cultures, too many backstories, too many relationships, too much history. I can't keep everything straight anymore. To finish the series, I really need Bridget's help."

"No," Derrick said flatly as he set the plate down on the nightstand. Bob actually ate fruit now, so it was mostly empty. "I'll just bring you all the previous books in the series. If you need to know something, try asking me. And if I don't remember, then you can look it up."

Bob sat down on the edge of the bed and picked up the plate. He'd learned not to butt heads with Derrick. It just made the boy stubborn. "But a lot of times I'm not exactly sure where or when I've said things. That will take hours. Instead of writing, I'll be sitting here skimming thousands of pages. Bridget has this huge cross-referenced database. Without it, I'm going to make mistakes." He tried for a connection. "You know how fans are. Change a character's eye color, and they start obsessing it's a hint it's not the same character at all."

"Like the were-fox," Derrick said.

"Right. The fans will never forgive me for that one." In *King of Swords*, Bob had said a character named Sonder Cozen was a were-fox. By the time Sonder popped up again in *Mountains of the Moon*, Bob's faulty memory had decided he was a were-lynx, a mistake neither the editor nor the copyeditor caught. After *Mountains of the Moon* came out, complaints and speculation had dominated the Swords and Shadows Reddit for weeks. "So if you could let me borrow your phone, I can email Bridget some questions." He peeled back the lid of the entree. Today it was two tiny pieces of chicken covered with a yellow sauce and flecked with a few bits of red pepper. Next to them was approximately a quarter-cup of white rice. He picked up his plastic fork and dug in. After weeks of limited food and limitless treadmill, he was now about the size he'd been in college.

The boy made a scoffing noise. "Right. In two seconds, you'd be dialing 911."

"I promise I won't. Come on, Derrick, I need Bridget's help." It wasn't even a lie. Bob did need Bridget. To save him. "I can't finish without her." He spoke around a mouthful of food. "There's no way I can write thousands of words tying up all the loose ends from the six previous books without having access to her. Plus she's got all these reference works about medieval royalty and feasting and child-rearing practices. Do you want a book larded with mistakes? I need her."

"Is that why those chapters you showed me yesterday didn't seem as good as some of the other books?"

Feeling a twist of offense, Bob made himself nod. "Right. Because I could only rely on my memory."

"All right." Derrick sighed. "Type up the questions you want me to send her."

"Thank you," Bob said as he scraped up the last of the gummy food from the plastic box. "I'll get my thoughts organized."

Lying in bed that night, Bob tried to figure out how to alert Bridget.

His first idea was to refer to Princess Elspeth, King Tristan's daughter. In *Darkest Heart* she'd been kidnapped by Maulty Minglehouse, forced to marry him in front of a drunken, bribed priest. A nobleman fallen on hard times, Maulty had erroneously thought that the marriage might make King Tristan elevate him to a higher position. Instead, the king, believing his own daughter had defied him, and fearing that marked her as the murderer foretold by the blind seer, had sent assassins after them.

But invoking Elspeth seemed too big a clue. While Bridget knew the books better than anyone, Derrick was nearly as familiar. Any mention of Elspeth, and Bob's email wouldn't get sent. Any mention of Elspeth, and Derrick might tell his mother, at which point Joanne might decide it was time to make Bob disappear.

He had to choose his words carefully, the exact opposite of the technique that had allowed him to write two books and nearly finish one.

Whatever he wrote would be turned into ones and zeros on a computer. That meant he couldn't write in lemon juice (which he didn't have) or urine (which he did, unfortunately, thanks to the chamber pot) in the hopes Bridget would hold the paper over a candle flame to reveal its secrets.

And of course Derrick wouldn't transmit anything that was clearly a code, such as a nonsense string of numbers, letters, or words.

Bridget was Bob's only hope, but getting her to understand he was in trouble seemed nearly impossible. The only thing in Bob's favor was that she was so smart. So watchful. And so surprisingly brave. He would never forget her facing down the crowd at Powell's.

Finally, Bob realized how he could get her to look underneath the surface of his note. In the middle of the night, he got up, snugged the quilt against the door, switched on the lamp and rolled a piece of paper into the typewriter. It took several tries to get it right. He kept blinking and yawning. But finally he had a message that might pass muster with Derrick while still alerting Bridget.

Looking at the finished product, he sighed. Because he also knew that it might hurt her.

BRIDGET

A Rabble Approaching

"I won't let anyone hurt you again." King Orwen gathered Jancy into his arms.

With a gasp, she went rigid. But when he did nothing more, her shoulders slowly relaxed. She tilted her head back to return his gaze.

His focus narrowed until there was only her. Did Jancy have any idea how beautiful she was, with her black curls tumbling past her shoulders? Her generous mouth, ripe for kissing?

His gaze went from her full lips to her sky-blue eyes and back again. And she was doing the same to him, looking from eyes to lips to eyes to—

"Sire!" A page burst into the room. "Sire!"

Releasing Jancy, King Orwen turned, warmth replaced by cold fury. "Did I not make it clear I was not to be disturbed?" His hand dropped to the hilt of his sword. He was torn between taking the flat to the boy's backside or simply running him through.

The page's face paled until the only color was the spots on his forehead and cheeks. "Begging your pardon, Sire, but there is a rabble approaching." He *drew a shaky breath. "And they are demanding your head."*

With a sigh, Bridget closed *Mountains of the Moon.* She gave the book a pat to thank it. She'd read it a dozen times, but that ending never failed to thrill her.

For a long moment, Ajay didn't move. Didn't even seem to breathe. Then he shook his head as if waking from a dream. "Wait. What?"

"That's the end of the last book." Reading aloud the scene between Jancy and King Orwen, Bridget had imagined herself and Ajay. What would it be like to have his arms around her? To feel him press his lips against her throat? Every day he sat right next to her, close enough that she could feel his warmth. He seemed like a miniature furnace, while she was always bouncing her knees, snugging her coat tighter, and occasionally blowing on her fingers. And every day he did not move a millimeter closer.

"You've been saying all week that this would be the last day, but that can't be the end," Ajay protested. "He can't just leave us hanging there. That's got to be the peasant army coming for King Orwen, right? What's going to happen when Jancy learns that Rowan's leading it? Plus, don't the humans realize they have to stop fighting each other and start fighting the undead? It's almost too late! And the unicorns still haven't said if they'll help."

"Welcome to how everyone else has felt for the last three-plus years." Bridget popped the last spoonful of her mulligatawny soup into her mouth. She was trying to hide it, but she felt equally bereft, for different reasons.

Tomorrow was the last day before winter break. When school started up again in January, would Ajay still want to eat with her, now that their reason for being together was finished?

She had been counting on their trade lasting well into the new year, but then Ajay had come back from Thanksgiving break and admitted he'd just listened to the audiobook of *Court of Sorrows*. He had been so apologetic, but then again, he was always so polite. Had it just been a way of shortening their time together without coming right out and saying it? Even now, she was still unsure how much his presence next to her was due to her and how much was due to the books. Maybe she could start reading him another series. Although nothing was as good as Swords and Shadows.

Ajay persisted. "But you're not everyone else, are you? I know Bob sometimes asks you about what's he's already written. That must give you some pretty good clues about the next book."

Bob had asked her not to disclose his writer's block. Bridget settled for something true that wasn't the truth. "I haven't heard from him in a few weeks." Saying it aloud made her realize just how long it had been. What was supposed to be a distraction for Ajay became a concern for her. "Actually, that's the longest he's ever gone without asking about anything. That's not like him."

"Maybe he's found his groove, then."

"Maybe," she echoed, still feeling uneasy.

Ajay reached into his backpack. "Before the bell rings, I wanted to give you this." He pulled out a small flat package wrapped in blue paper printed with white snowflakes. The wrapping paper was a little crooked, like he'd done it himself.

"Oh," Bridget stammered, her mouth suddenly dry. "I didn't get you anything."

"I wasn't expecting anything. I just wanted to show my appreciation for you introducing me to some amazing people—even if they're fictional."

The package was too small for a book. Was that good or bad? A book could be a sign Ajay wanted to continue their reading ritual. But Bridget also wanted something that made it clear how he felt about her. That would make it obvious he liked her as much as she liked him.

What could be inside? Bold earrings that would brush her shoulders? Two tickets to an upcoming concert or play? A charm on a delicate silver chain?

Inside Bridget's chest, her heart started to gallop. Warmth suffused her whole body. For once, she didn't even feel the cold. She tried to slide her finger underneath the tape, but the paper tore.

She lifted the lid of the box to reveal something nestled in white tissue paper.

A pair of socks. Thick, plain, black wool socks.

"Oh," she said, suddenly feeling like an idiot. "Thank you."

Mercifully, the bell rang, signaling the end of lunch and giving her the out she so desperately needed. Tears stung her eyes as she realized just how stupid she'd been, making up a romantic story about what was clearly their practical, transactional relationship. Grabbing up the socks, the book, and her pack, she made toward the doors into the cafeteria as fast as she could.

"Bridget—wait!"

"Sorry!" she called without turning around. "I'm late for a test."

BOB

False Words

Hello Bridget—
You'll be glad to know I've turned my attention back
to the manuscript and am making good progress.
Have you had a chance to ask your parents about
working for me full-time over the summer? Please
tell Anna and Graham how much I'll need your help
if I'm to finish.

As we discussed earlier, I'm adding a new
character. So please look for all instances of:
   "Jade Tarnno."
And then flag each spot with:
   "Add Ken Pipem."
The rest of this letter details what I'm trying to
get right on my third attempt, at least initially.

Can you help with researching endowments?
Can you look up whether daughters can be
inheritors of the nation? Consider the monarchy—
what if Tristan learned that he and Princess
Ofelia were not only father and daughter but
also cousins because of a secret wedding?
Bridget, that means I will probably need some

more help with adding extra characters too, like jongleur Ken Pipem.

Best,

Bob

Derrick looked up from the note Bob had typed up last night. "Who's this Jade Tarnno person? And Ken Pipem?"

"Jade Tarnno is a female minstrel I'll be adding to the book," Bob said, improvising madly. "She has green eyes and black hair as straight as a waterfall. Her lover is a jongleur named Ken Pipem. Ken is always masked because he's hiding his leprosy." Behind his hand, he stifled a burp. "Ken wears a mask to hide his deformed nose, and the fingers of his left glove are stuffed with horsehair to hide the fact that two are missing."

As Bob frantically lied to save himself, Jade Tarnno and Ken Pipem took shape in his imagination. Took shape and then broke out of the mold. They were no longer flat characters he'd just made up.

Instead, it felt like he was describing people who already existed. Like he was watching a movie and simply describing what he saw.

This vision was also informed by his years of research. In medieval times there had been more than two thousand leper colonies in France alone. The Sunday after the leper was diagnosed, he was dressed in a shroud and brought to church on a litter carried by four priests singing psalms. Once inside, he was set down a safe distance from the congregation. After the service for the dead was read, the priests carried him out of town to the leper colony. He was given a bell or a pair of castanets to warn others of his presence. And he could never again enter a church, a mill, a market, or any place where others gathered. He could not bathe himself nor wash his clothes in stream nor spring. If anyone spoke to him on the road, he could not answer until he was downwind.

Derrick interrupted Bob's thoughts. "How come leprosy was a thing back then but it's not now?"

"Red squirrels can carry leprosy, and at the time there was a huge trade in both red squirrel meat and fur. There is a theory that's how it spread. And now we have antibiotics that can cure it."

This was all true. But it was also false, meant to lull Derrick.

The boy nodded. "I'll email her today. How long do you think it will take her to answer?"

If Bridget didn't understand it, he didn't need Derrick immediately seeing a puzzled reply and figuring out what Bob had done. "I'm asking for a lot of research, so no point in checking back for at least a few days."

After Derrick left, Bob kept thinking about the letter. Not about whether Bridget might decipher his hidden messages, but about the false words hiding the true ones. What if familial relationships in the kingdom were more tangled than he'd depicted? Readers ate that stuff up. He'd definitely add them to the version he was writing for Derrick.

He stifled another burp. Last night, to make sure

Derrick never found the two earlier drafts of the note he'd worked on, he'd carried them both to bed.

And then in the darkness Bob had slowly torn off bits of paper, put them into his mouth, chewed, and swallowed.

BRIDGET

Not Completely Following

Sitting at the dining room table, Bridget rubbed her eyes and read Bob's email for the millionth time. She took another sip of coffee. Maybe the reason she couldn't follow it was because she was too tired. It felt like she'd been awake all night, coming to terms with the reality of what her relationship with Ajay was. Practical. Transactional. She had read him books. In return, he'd provided her with lunch and a pair of socks. Anything more than that had been just in her pathetic imagination.

When she'd finally dragged herself out of her twisted sheets, Bob's message was waiting in her email inbox. It was a relief to think of something else. The first sentence made sense. Bob was working on *Eyes of the Forest* again. That was good. She lifted another spoonful of Wheaties to her mouth. And he wanted her to work for him full-time over the summer. That was great. The money could go into her college fund.

At least it would be great if Bob meant it. If he was mentally competent when he'd written it. Because before the part about her working for him came the sentence about how she should talk to her parents about it.

Bob knew her mom was dead. They had talked about it a few times. Once he had said something about understanding how big a hole someone could leave in your life. How could he have forgotten something so major?

Not to mention that her mom's name had been Vivian, not Anna. Just like her dad was named Jim, not Graham.

Setting that strangeness aside for a moment, Bridget moved on to the rest of the note. Bob hadn't said anything to her before about adding a new character. The names Jade Tarnno and Ken Pipem meant nothing to her. But then the world of Swords and Shadows was far more real to Bob than this one. What was an oblique mention from her point of view might have amounted to whole paragraphs or even chapters in his, stories that were only in his head and not yet on paper.

As she took her last bite of cereal, Bridget opened up her database and did a quick search. First for *Jade Tarnno*. Then just for *Jade*. She found some mentions of the color jade, but not the person.

Color. Bridget paused. That was a whole facet of the series she hadn't captured. It gave her a new reason to reread the books. She brought herself back to the task at hand. No Pipems. The few instances of the word *Ken* were in the archaic sense of "to know."

She closed her laptop and went to her room. As she got dressed, she mulled over the rest of Bob's email. How could King Tristan be anything more than Princess Ofelia's father? Cousins shared grandparents. She tried to figure it out, but failed. Of course, anything was possible in the Swords and Shadows series. Maybe Bob would introduce time traveling in *Eyes of the Forest*.

Bridget grabbed her coat and backpack, then locked the door behind her. As she walked to the bus, the uncomfortable feeling that something wasn't right kept nagging her.

At the stop, she took out her phone and reread the email. She made herself pull back and consider it as a whole. It didn't make a lot of sense. And it didn't really sound like Bob. Or rather, it sort of did, but a hyped-up Bob. A confused Bob.

She hit the REPLY button. "Bob?" Her thumbs hesitated before she finally started typing. "Are you all right? I'm not completely following you."

In between classes, she kept checking her email, but Bob did not reply. Trying to figure out what was wrong with him made it easier for her to walk into physics, to see Ajay again now that she knew how he viewed her.

"Can I talk to you at lunch?" she asked. She needed to discuss it with someone, and Ajay was really her only choice.

"Sure." Ajay's dark eyes sparked in a way that would have made her stomach flip just the day before. "I even brought two tiffin boxes today."

AJAY

What's the Worst That Can Happen?

All through Mr. Manning's class, Ajay kept his eye on Bridget. She had been upset yesterday, but today she wanted to have lunch with him. That should have been a relief, but it wasn't really. Maybe she just wanted to yell at him about the socks.

Ajay had wanted to give a gift to Bridget. But what? And then it had come to him. The weather was only going to get colder, but she was already always cold. Especially her feet. No matter how much she jigged her legs, she frequently complained about losing feelings in her toes.

So he had bought her a pair of the heaviest black knee socks he could find, knit from New Zealand wool, which the clerk at Nordstrom had assured him was the best kind, and not the least bit itchy.

The price had been surprisingly high. But only the best for Bridget.

Except judging by the look she had given him yesterday when she saw what was inside the box, she didn't see it the same way. It was clear he had made some awful mistake.

He tried to pay attention to Mr. Manning as class

dragged by. When it finally ended, they walked in silence to what Ajay now thought of as "their" table. He opened his backpack and handed her a tiffin box.

"So what did you want to talk about?" He braced himself.

"I got a very strange message from Bob yesterday. I don't know what to think." She handed over her phone.

Relief rolled over him. He felt nearly reverent as he regarded it. "Wow! So this is from the great man himself?"

"Yes, but read it and tell me what you think."

Ajay read the message once, quickly. Then he scrolled back up to the top and read it over again, more slowly. Finally he looked at Bridget.

His mouth twisted. "Doesn't he know that your mom is, um, dead?"

"He has to. We've talked about it. But that's not even the weirdest thing. Neither of those names are actually my parents'."

Ajay jerked his head back. "They aren't named Anna and Graham?"

"Vivian and James."

He blinked. "That's a lot different."

"And all those questions he asks about the series. I don't know any of the answers. I don't even understand most of them."

Trying to think of another explanation, he asked, "Does he have another researcher he got you mixed up with?" Although who could mix Bridget up with anyone?

"I'm the only one." Taking the phone back, she looked

at his words again. "And if you take everything together, it just plain doesn't make sense. It doesn't even really sound like Bob."

Ajay tried to put it delicately. "Do you think he could have had a little too much holiday cheer?"

She wrinkled her nose. "In interviews, he always says that he doesn't drink."

Ajay made a humming noise. "That doesn't mean he couldn't have started." Then he said carefully, "Do you think maybe he's having some medical problem? I mean, after all, he's kind of a rotund guy." If his sister were here, she would know exactly what high-risk categories Bob fell into. Maybe he'd had a stroke or was getting Alzheimer's. Because something had definitely scrambled Bob's wires.

"I've got his phone number." Taking the phone back, Bridget scrolled around until she found it. Her finger hovered over the button. "I'm going to call him."

Ajay watched her face as she listened to the ringing. When it stopped, he faintly heard a man's voice. A recording.

"Bob," she said slowly, "this is Bridget. Can you call me? I just have a question about your email." After reciting her phone number, she pressed the button to end the call.

"My grandma had Parkinson's," Ajay said. "She got things confused. A few times she even hallucinated." Tears sparked his eyes at her memory. "Have you ever seen one of his hands trembling?"

"No." She exhaled heavily. "But I haven't seen him in person for a long time."

"Does Bob have a friend you could call? Someone you could ask to check on him?"

"He must have friends," she said, her tone uncertain. "But I don't know them or even who they are. We only ever talked about the books."

"Do you know where he lives?"

"About twenty miles outside of Portland. It's pretty private. I've only been there once, with my dad. Bob bought the acreage on either side so he wouldn't have to deal with neighbors."

"Okay," Ajay said. "How about this? If you haven't heard from him by the last bell, I say we go out there." He would think of some excuse to text his mom, ideally something about studying.

Her expression brightened. "You don't think I'm overreacting?"

He shook his head. "The part about your parents is too weird. And even if it is an overreaction, what's the worst that can happen? He'll explain, and we'll leave." It was a relief that they were a team again. "We can take an Uber or something."

Bridget straightened up. "We can take my dad's car."

DERRICK

A Sense of Unreality

Something had happened yesterday between Bridget and Ajay. Derrick's heart had sunk at the sight of Ajay's present as he watched them through the cafeteria window. But whatever was inside had not brought a smile to Bridget's face. Instead, she had looked like she was ... hurt? Was that the right word?

And last night, when Bob had asked him to send the message to her, something about that pained emotion as well as her bland reaction to when he had mentioned Bob had reassured Derrick that it was okay to send the message. Derrick had also decided it was wiser not to consult his mom beforehand. Better to ask for forgiveness than permission.

Today, Bridget walked into physics class, not downcast, but rather animated. Quick movements, an urgent hissed conversation with Ajay. And then they ate lunch together, an activity Derrick had hoped would become a thing of the past. But the first thing Bridget did was hand Ajay her phone.

Derrick took out his own phone, already feeling dread

and anger meet in his stomach, forming a pit of acid. And then he logged in to Bob's email box.

A sense of unreality filled Derrick as he read Bridget's confused reply. It was clear Bob's message had been more than it appeared. How could he have been so stupid? How could he have fallen for Bob's lies? The man was a professional storyteller, after all.

But what had Bob said to her? Were the police even now at the cabin, breaking down the door? Jumping to his feet, Derrick dumped his half-eaten meal in the trash. He would ditch school. Something he had never done before, but then again, he had never kidnapped anyone before either.

Five minutes later, he was in his car and on his way to the cabin. The entire hour he lectured himself and rehearsed what he would say to Bob, his mom, and any law enforcement.

Finally he was turning on Hoot Owl Road. Even though there were no police cruisers in front of the cabin, he was still filled with anxiety. He unlocked the door, and in a dozen quick steps, he was down the hall. He burst into Bob's room. The old man was clacking away at the typewriter, so engrossed he didn't register Derrick's entrance until he slammed the door.

Reaching past him, Derrick pounded his fist on the OFF button on the treadmill.

Coasting to a stop, Bob heaved a sigh. "What do you need me to do this time? Shake my booty? Read someone's awful poem?"

Derrick's hands were clenched around the phone so tightly his fingers hurt. "You lied to me!"

"What?" Bob widened his rheumy eyes, trying to look innocent.

Derrick shook the phone at him. "Bridget emailed you back this morning, but I only just now saw it. You said you needed her help researching. But you must have really wanted her help escaping!"

"That's not true." The old man shook his head.

"Then why did she ask if you were okay and say she didn't understand what you were talking about? What message did you hide in that email you had me send?" And what would his mom say when she found out?

Bob raised his hands. "Bridget's just rusty because it's been a long time since I gave her anything to work with. She's forgotten things."

Derrick ground his teeth at the lies. "I trusted you, and you betrayed me!"

Bob raised his open hands. "I swear to you that nothing nefarious is going on! Bridget just doesn't remember some of the details. It's been months since I worked on the book."

"If she doesn't remember it, why not just say so? Instead, she's worried about you. She thinks you're not making sense. Even if she doesn't figure out whatever secret message you hid in there, she's still concerned. You have to help me think of something to say that will make her stop asking questions."

Bob's white eyebrows, thick as caterpillars, drew

together. "Maybe tell her I was drinking? Or sleep deprived?"

Both ideas were so lame Derrick didn't even bother responding to them.

The phone vibrated in his hand, startling him so much he jerked. The display read *Mom*.

Oh crap. Even Bob appeared dismayed at the sight.

"Hello?" Derrick's voice cracked.

"Check the video feed from Bob's house. There's two kids in front of the gate."

"They're probably just fans."

"It sounds like they know something."

After putting his finger on his lips and waiting until Bob nodded understanding, he put his mom on speakerphone and then pulled up the feeds from the security cameras from Bob's house. A Subaru was parked in front of the gate. Two people were peering in between the wrought-iron curlicues. When the smaller one stepped closer to the light, he saw red hair.

Derrick said, "It's not just two kids." He glared down at Bob, resisting the urge to kick him. "One's Bridget, his researcher."

His mom's voice sharpened. "And why would she be there?" Without waiting for an answer, she said, "The security system already dispatched the police. I don't know if I can beat them there."

BRIDGET

Tilting Off Its Axis

Welcome to our humble abode!" Bridget made a sweeping gesture as she stepped in the front door. Her breakfast dishes were in the sink, not the dishwasher, and there was a huge pile of mail on the dining room table, but things were mostly picked up, for which she was secretly thankful.

She tried to see her house through Ajay's eyes. The olive green L-shaped couch with the gray-and-orange throw pillows. The long black leather ottoman in front of the couch that doubled as both footrest and coffee table. Opposite the couch, her dad's gray overstuffed chair was flanked by a floor lamp standing on three carved wooden legs.

Other than the addition of framed photos of her mom or their family, Bridget realized everything looked just the way it had when her mom was still alive. The room suddenly felt like a time capsule—or a museum.

Darting down the hallway to her room, Bridget tossed her pack on her bed and quickly closed the door as she left. It was already weird enough being alone with Ajay without him seeing her unmade bed or the clothes that had missed the hamper.

But he was still in the living room, focused on the framed photo of a grinning girl on a skateboard. He pointed. "So that's you?"

"My mom, actually." In the picture, her mom was a few years younger than Bridget was now. She wore a yellow T-shirt, and her red hair curled up over the edge of her helmet. Her smile was so big it squeezed her eyes closed. "She was more daring than I'll ever be. She wasn't scared of anything." Except dying, but there wasn't really a way to talk about that.

"You look a lot like her. And I'll bet your personalities are more alike than you think."

Bridget didn't argue, even though the only way they were really alike was their shared love of Swords and Shadows. Instead, she went into the kitchen and grabbed the Subaru's keys from a hook. She was allowed to use the car for grocery shopping or anything that required her to haul cargo or be out after dark—or for emergencies. And this definitely felt like one.

Once they were in the car, Bridget's feeling that the world was tilting off its axis continued. Yesterday learning that her feelings for Ajay were one-sided. Today receiving Bob's odd message. Then seeing her house and her mom through Ajay's eyes. And now she was driving him to Bob's in her dad's car, the two of them sealed off from the world in a capsule made of glass and steel. All the parts of her life were coming together in ways she'd never expected.

"When was the last time you were at his house?" Ajay asked as she merged onto the highway.

"It was just that once, right after I met him. My dad wanted to make sure he was normal."

Ajay made a humming sound. "I guess I'd wonder about some grown man who wanted to hire my twelve-year-old daughter."

"Well, Bob's not normal, but he's definitely not creepy. And my dad was relieved when he realized Bob wanted to do it all by email. For the first couple of years, he occasionally read Bob's emails to make sure he wasn't sneaking any weird things in. Which he wasn't."

"So back up—you've only been to his house once, and you remember how to get there?"

"I have a good memory." She felt oddly defensive. "It's why Bob hired me in the first place."

The farther they got from the city, the more things spread out. Huge houses on acreage alternated with farm fields that lay fallow at this time of year.

By memory, she turned down one road and then, a mile later, another. Now there weren't any other cars on the road besides her dad's. But when Bridget turned into Bob's driveway, she had to hit her brakes. What had once been a long road was now bisected by a black wrought-iron gate.

"This wasn't here before."

AJAY

Put Your Hands in the Air

The gate was about eight feet high, made of wrought iron twisted into abstract shapes. In the middle of each swinging gate was a large *S* set in a circle. And then Ajay realized the shapes were really wings and horns, echoing the unicorns in Swords and Shadows.

Bridget turned off the engine, and they got out of the car. The air was still and cold around them. Ajay felt oddly small and exposed.

On the left side of the gate was a keypad. Bridget pushed the intercom button underneath, but no one answered. Ajay pressed his face to the gate, peering through the gathering darkness. "There's two cars parked in front," he told her. "A pickup and a Tesla."

Bridget pressed the button again. This time she waved at the camera. But still no crackle broke the silence.

She stepped back to consider the gate and the brick walls on either side. "There's got to be a way to get in."

Ajay shuffled his feet. Was that really their place? "Maybe instead we should call the police?"

"And tell them what? That Bob sent me an email and got my parents' names wrong? We need more than that.

And what if he's passed out inside?" Bridget stuck her head and then her shoulders through the curve of the S. She pulled back. "If I take off my coat, I think I can squeeze through here." She was already unzipping it. She laid it on the ground next to the gate.

"There's no way I can. But I don't want you going up to the house by yourself." Ajay stepped back and eyed the brick wall. It was about seven feet tall. "I think if I got a running start I could jump and pull myself up."

Bridget pointed her arms like a diver and started wriggling through the S. She got caught at the hips, but she kept wiggling, and finally she slipped through. Getting back on her feet, she pulled her coat through the gate.

"Okay, wait for me." Ajay walked backward a dozen steps, then launched himself into a run. He leapt, and his fingers found gritty purchase. With trembling arms, he managed to pull himself up and get one knee and then the other on top of the wall. By the time he thought about the possibility of broken glass, it was too late. But the top of the wall was just concrete, nothing more.

He swiveled around and jumped down from a sitting position, landing with his knees bent. Then together he and Bridget walked to the front door. It had a gryphon-head iron knocker as well as a bell. They tried both, but no one came to the door. Ajay pressed his ear against the cold wood, but heard nothing.

By unspoken agreement, they began to move around the perimeter of the house, using their phone flashlights to peer in each room. They were clean and tidy. They struck Ajay as almost sterile, as if no one lived here at all.

"It's hard to think of the guy who wrote Swords and Shadows living in a McMansion with wall-to-wall carpeting," he whispered. They were both whispering now, even though their stated purpose was to attract Bob's attention.

"And there's not even a single fireplace you could roast a stag in," Bridget whispered back.

His breath caught when his flashlight spotlighted a man all dressed in silver. "What's that?"

Bridget pressed her face next to his, staring through the gap in the curtains.

She exhaled. "Oh, that's just a suit of armor. I remember it from when I came here. That's Bob's office."

Suddenly a bright light lit up the gloom behind them. Ajay turned, shading his eyes with his hand.

"This is the police!" a man yelled. "Put your hands in the air. Now!"

BRIDGET

Imposter

"Do it! Now!" the cop yelled at Bridget and Ajay from the other side of the gate. "Get your hands where I can see them."

Trembling, Bridget raised both hands over her head, squinting in the powerful glare of the cop's flashlight.

He tapped a code on the keypad. The gate clicked as it unlocked. He shouldered it aside and walked toward them. Bridget's heart sped up. His right hand rested on the butt of his gun.

"This is private property. You're trespassing." He moved his flashlight from their faces and played it along the side of the house.

"We're not burglars," Bridget said. Her heart was a drum in her chest.

"I'm the one asking questions here."

Hands still raised, she and Ajay exchanged a glance. It didn't seem like a good time to mention she hadn't actually asked a question.

He turned back to them. "How did you get in?"

"I crawled through one of the *S*'s," Bridget said.

"What?" He sounded irritated.

"The *S*'s in the middle of the gate." After a second, she added, "Sir."

"And I climbed over the wall," Ajay said.

"Didn't you two stop to think that the gate and the walls are there for a reason? Trespassing is a crime."

"But we're not trespassing!" she protested. "We're here because we're worried about Bob."

"You mean Mr. Haldon?"

"Yes. Bob. Mr. Haldon. I'm his research assistant."

"That's a new one," the cop said. "*Research assistant.*" He gave her words a mocking spin. "You're a teenager."

With difficulty, Bridget kept the tremble from her voice. "I'm a teenager, *and* I'm his research assistant. And last night he sent me this weird garbled message and then didn't answer when I asked if he was okay."

"Uh-huh. And how did he send this message? Through the TV? Or by wearing certain colors in a photo?"

The cop wasn't making sense. "What? He emailed me. If you look at his message, you'll see what I mean." Bridget started to lower one hand toward her phone.

"Keep your hands where I can see them! Do not reach in your pockets." He let out an irritated sigh.

Belatedly, Bridget realized why he was asking such strange questions. "You think we're just obsessed fans. That we don't really know him. But that's not true!"

The flashlight shifted focus to Ajay's face. "So you know Mr. Haldon as well?"

Ajay cleared his throat. "Well, actually, it's just Bridget

who does. But she showed me his message. And she does work for him."

The cop's skeptical expression hadn't changed. "And how do you know that?"

"Well, uh, she knows everything about his books. And she's always working on this database for him."

"What do you mean?" the cop asked.

"It's like an index to the facts in the Swords and Shadows series," she said. If the cop considered Bob's complicated world for a second, he'd understand. "Have you ever read any of the books?"

"No." He bit off the word.

"Then you've probably watched the TV show." That was pretty much a given. It was one of the most popular shows in America.

"I only watch sports."

He certainly wasn't giving her much to work with. "Okay. Well, everything in Swords and Shadows is really detailed. It's a fantasy world with a lot of layers. A few years ago, Bob, um, Mr. Haldon, hired me to keep track of all those details. And when he's writing, he'll ask me questions about what he's already established so there's continuity between books."

The cop didn't look convinced. At all. "If you work for him, why did you need to break in?"

"First of all, we were not breaking in. We were just looking in the windows to make sure he hadn't collapsed or something." As Bridget spoke, a second police SUV pulled up at the gate. "And I don't work here. I work at my house, and we communicate by email."

"Yeah, yeah, right," he said as the second officer walked toward them. She was a dark-haired woman who might have looked friendly if she smiled.

She wasn't smiling. "What've you got?"

"Two kids who claim they're just worried about Haldon's health. Can you pat them down for me?"

She did, starting with Ajay. When it was Bridget's turn, she tried to think of it as a particularly vigorous massage.

"They're both clean," the female cop said as she stepped back. "Either of you two have ID?" When they nodded, she said, "Let's see it."

Ajay pulled out his wallet and handed it to her. She read aloud as she scribbled in a notebook she'd taken from her pocket. "Ajay Kapoor. Age seventeen. Lives in Southwest Portland."

"Are you arresting us?" Bridget's voice shook. Without answering the question, the cop handed Ajay's ID back, then held out her hand for Bridget's.

She pulled out her phone case, which also had slots for her ID.

"Bridget Shepherd," the cop read. "Also seventeen. Also lives in Southwest Portland."

When the woman handed her phone back, Bridget said, "Can I show you the message I got?" Was she imagining it, or was Ajay shaking his head? Besides, it was too late, because the cops were shrugging.

After she opened the message, they both glanced at it.

"So?" the female cop said.

"So it doesn't make any sense. Like, those names aren't my parents' names."

"This isn't even from Haldon," the male cop said as he clicked on the email address. "It's from someone named TheWorldOfSwordsAndShadows@gmail.com."

"That's him," Bridget said. "That's his email address. B—Mr. Haldon told me he tried to get KingOfSwords or SwordsAndShadows but they were both taken."

The female cop made a scoffing noise. "Don't they teach you guys basic internet literacy? On the internet, anyone can be anyone."

"Have either of you been drinking or using drugs?" the male cop asked.

"No, sir," she said. Ajay echoed her.

A black Honda pulled in between her dad's Subaru and the first cop's SUV. There were now four cars lined up in front of the gate. The woman who got out looked like she was in her early forties. Clutching her calf-length fur coat closed at the throat, she walked briskly over to them.

"Hey, Joanne," the male cop said over his shoulder.

"Ms. Dart," the female cop said.

She nodded. "Officer Albright. Officer Rubio." Her eyelashes were so lush they looked like fur. Her blond shoulder-length hair was elaborately styled, and jewels gleamed on her ears and fingers. "Whatcha got this time?"

"A couple of teenagers. Know these two?"

She shook her head. "I've never seen either of them before in my life."

He pursed his lips. "This one says she works for Mr. Haldon as his researcher."

"His researcher?" Her laugh was a bark. "That's a new

one." She looked closer at Bridget. "I guess you're too young to claim you're his wife or girlfriend."

"What?" Bridget said. "Of course not. He's old enough to be my grandfather."

Officer Rubio shook her head. "Do you realize how many fans show up here? Why do you think he has a security system? The benign ones just want his autograph or a chance to talk to him. And some think he loves them, or that he would if he just met them."

"Except for that guy who was sure he was an imposter who killed the real Haldon," Officer Albright interjected. The three adults all made faces.

"I *am* his researcher!" Bridget wasn't scared any longer. She was exasperated. "And I do work for him. He sent me this weird message, and I just want to make sure he's okay."

Joanne shrugged. "Well, I've worked as his personal assistant for six months, and I've never heard of you. All I know is I'm getting tired of this. All these so-called fans showing up at all hours, half the time in weird costumes. At least you're dressed normal. Last month, there was some guy who'd had plastic surgery on his ears to make him look more like this elf named Car Umlaut or something."

"Car Umass," Bridget corrected. He'd played a key role in both *Darkest Heart* and *Unicorn Wars*.

"Whatever." Joanne waved a hand. "I've never read any of the books. I have better things to do with my life."

As Officer Albright nodded in agreement, Ajay said mildly, "It seems like Haldon makes a good living at it."

"Good enough he can fly off to Flanders and look at castles," Joanne said. "Which is where he is right now."

"Nice work if you can get it," Officer Albright said. He and Officer Rubio exchanged a look. "So tell me the truth, you two. Were you just trying to get a look at your favorite author's home?"

Before Bridget could say anything, Ajay rushed in. "I'm sorry, officers. You're right. We shouldn't have done it. And I apologize that we did."

Realizing he was attempting to extricate them, Bridget closed her mouth.

Officer Rubio looked at Joanne. "I've got their names and addresses in case you discover any damage after you get inside. But if you don't, do you still want to press charges?"

"I think they've learned their lesson." Joanne gave them a sour smile. "But if they show up here again, all that changes."

AJAY

A Real Friend

The car was silent as they drove away from Bob's house. Ajay was half turned away from Bridget, looking out the passenger side window. He didn't want to, but he was busy recalculating. Trying to think with his head and not his heart, the way Aprita had said.

Finally, Bridget broke the silence. "I still think something's wrong." Her voice simmered with frustration.

Ajay sighed. "If there is, I don't see what you can do about it. I mean, you already emailed him, and he hasn't answered. If there really is something wrong with his health, hopefully someone in Flanders can help him."

"Flanders!" Bridget slapped the steering wheel. "You didn't really believe that Joanne person, did you?"

Instead of answering, Ajay reluctantly gave voice to one of the thoughts crowding his head. "Joanne didn't even know about you."

Bridget huffed. "Well, I didn't know about her, so we're even. Besides, why should Bob tell me about her or vice versa? We represent completely different aspects of his life."

"I guess you're right." But he was just placating her.

His heart protested, but his brain overruled it. "But I have to say I didn't *not* believe Joanne. I mean, it makes sense. Why wouldn't Bob go to Flanders? You've talked about how much research he does. So he's probably just jet-lagged. Which would explain the mistakes in his message."

After a long pause, Bridget said, "I'm starting to think they're not mistakes."

"Then what are they?"

"Clues."

Every word of hers was just making Ajay feel worse. "Clues to what, Bridget? If Bob had something he wanted to tell you, why wouldn't he just come out and say it?"

She stopped at a red light. "I don't know. But I think something's wrong."

He ran a hand down his face. His fingers were still trembling. "We're just lucky those cops didn't arrest us. I was imagining having to call my parents from the police station. Even in my imagination, it didn't go over well." His parents had reluctantly accepted Ajay's B's. Encouraged his cooking. But an arrest? That would break their hearts.

"But we didn't do anything wrong." She turned back onto the highway. "All we did was look in the windows to make sure Bob wasn't hurt or passed out or something."

"You left out the part about how we got past the locked gate. Which *is* trespassing, at least technically." Ajay pinched the bridge of his nose, trying to find the right words. "You know, until we talked to those cops, I'd never thought about what it would be like being a celebrity. Having strangers show up at your house uninvited. Having some of them believe they're in love with you, or even that you're in love with them. But those people really think it's true." He focused on the two cones of light pushing ahead of them into the darkness.

Out of the corner of his eye, he saw how she stiffened. "You believe me, don't you?"

The silence stretched out until it seemed almost unbearable.

Finally, Ajay broke it. "Look, you clearly know everything about Swords and Shadows. More than it's possible to imagine anyone else in the world knowing. And I've seen you working on that database so many times." The cop's words echoed in his thoughts. *On the internet, anyone can be anyone.*

"So you don't believe Bob hired me! You don't believe I know him."

"I didn't say that, Bridget," Ajay finally said. "You did."

"But that's what you're thinking, isn't it? That actually I typed up Bob's message to myself? That doesn't even make sense."

But neither did that guy getting his ears surgically altered to look like an elf's, Ajay thought but didn't say. Finally, he sighed. "Can't we just go back to the way things were? I want to be your friend, Bridget. It seems like you need one."

"You make me sound like some charity case." She spit the words. "Not like a real friend. Don't worry. You don't have to keep earning brownie points by bringing me lunch and pretending to listen to me."

He finally shifted to face her. "Bridget, I honestly like

you. And I like you reading to me. These last few weeks have been great."

"You mean it was great until you figured out I'm just some mentally ill liar."

His phone buzzed, providing a welcome distraction, at least until he saw who it was. His mom. He bit his lip. He'd forgotten to tell her that he'd be home late. If he didn't answer, his mom would call every five minutes until he responded. And if he still didn't pick up, then she would probably demand the police put out an APB, as well as send his picture to Interpol and call the local news team.

"Hi, Mama," Ajay said brightly. He tapped his finger against his lips so that Bridget wouldn't say anything to give away her presence.

"Why are you not at home, son?"

"Sorry, I was um, in a study group. I'm on my way home. I know I'm getting a late start on dinner, but don't worry, I've got something fast in mind."

"Have you even packed?" She sounded tired.

"Mostly," he lied.

They said their goodbyes, and Ajay put his phone away. The car was dead silent, and the silence had a weight to it. The darkness pressed up against the windows. It was starting to rain. When Bridget turned on the wipers. Ajay was glad for a sound other than the tires' hum and the tapping of the rain. It felt like all the color had leached from the world. Everything was black or shades of gray.

"So how do I get to your house?" Her voice was matter-of-fact.

"You can just let me out on the corner of Thirtieth and Barbur. That would be the easiest."

Ajay waited for Bridget to argue, or to confront him about whom it would be "easiest" for and why. Instead, she just said, "Okay."

When she pulled up to the corner opposite the Chevron station, he said, "Look, Bridget, we'll talk about this more when I get back from Seattle, okay?"

Her voice was lifeless. "Sure."

After getting out, Ajay leaned in the open door. "I wish . . . ," he started, and then his words trailed off.

"Thank you for going to Bob's house with me," she said. "I really appreciate it." As she spoke, she let the car drift forward.

Ajay had to step back as the passenger door nearly closed itself. Then Bridget reached over and closed it the rest of the way.

In the streetlight, he saw a tear shining silver on her cheek.

BOB

Who's the Fool Now?

The room that was his prison cell had stopped existing for Bob. As he mechanically marched forward to nowhere, he no longer heard the treadmill's low whine, the slap of his feet, or the clack of the typewriter keys.

He no longer heard Derrick, out in the hall arguing on the phone with his mom.

Instead, he was with Jade Tarnno and Ken Pipem in the small bedchamber they'd been given as part of the king's entourage. They were accompanying King Orwen as he visited one of his dukes.

Bob knew he was taking a risk, writing pages to the real *Eyes of the Forest* before the boy went to bed, but he couldn't silence the story any longer. And maybe these pages could serve for both books, although he would have to retype them so he had two sets.

Bob was no longer trying to write badly. He was no longer trying at all. He hadn't felt like this for years, not since he wrote what became *King of Swords*. As if a narrator was whispering words in his ear as the scene played out in his mind's eye. All Bob had to do was put those words on paper.

Jade applied scent behind her ears and on her wrists. Lifting the hem of her skirt, she dabbed more perfume behind her knees.

Ken's voice was thin as parchment. "What are you doing?" Sitting on the edge of the bed, he fiddled with his black satin glove, trying to bend the horsehair-stuffed fingers into a more natural shape.

She straightened up and shook back her waterfall of hair. "Preparing for my audience with the king." She pinned a scrap of lace on top of her head. It was only a nod to propriety, as it did nothing to hide her hair.

"You appear to think the audience is going to occur in Orwen's bedchamber." Ken pushed back his jester's hood with its attached ears, leaving his mask in place. He even slept in it now. The story they put about was that Ken had been badly scarred by the pox. If the king knew what the mask hid, he would order him banished or even executed.

"It might." Jade's dark eyes were amused. "And would that be so bad?"

Ken imagined twisting the necklace around her throat. Twisting it until her face turned purple and she could no longer say such terrible things.

Instead, he took off his mask.

When the door behind him slammed, Bob jumped. He raised his head, blinking as the room came into focus.

"Everything's falling apart!" Derrick said. His face was flushed, his hands fisted. "And it's your fault."

"What?" Reluctantly, Bob hit the treadmill's OFF

button. The words describing Ken's disfigured face were already building up inside him, demanding release.

"Don't give me that. You know exactly what's wrong. That message you made me send Bridget must have been in code. Because she showed up at your house."

Bridget. Her name finally snapped him back to the here and now. "What happened?"

"She got past the gate and triggered the silent alarm. When the cops came, she told them she'd gotten a weird message from you and that she was worried you were having a stroke or something."

Bob realized he'd been too clever by half, disguising his words both too much and too little. He'd aroused Bridget's suspicions but not any useful action.

"Really?" he said mildly. "And then what happened?"

"The cops didn't really care. They just wrote off her and this guy she was with as crazy fans. But my mom met them at your house, and she *does* care. She told them you're traveling in Flanders looking at castles. She's really mad at you, and at me for being tricked by you."

Bob walked a tightrope of words. "I didn't trick you, Derrick. Those questions for Bridget are really things I need to know. Maybe I wasn't as clear as I could be because I'm not sleeping well. Just email Bridget back and say I'm in Europe doing research. Blame it on jet lag. Say I took an Ambien. Maybe even that I had a drink or two on top of that. Apologize if it was confusing and say I'll get back to her later. You can use any words you want. And that way you'll know there's no hidden messages."

"Right," Derrick said sarcastically. "Like I can trust

anything you say. You already fooled me once. You're going to have to pay for that. So who's the fool now?"

Who's the fool now? Could Ken say that to Jade, mocking her for believing King Orwen would give her anything without demanding a much higher price in return? Maybe he would even say it to her corpse. After all, it was rumored that some women summoned to visit the new king never made it out of his bedchamber alive.

Belatedly, Bob ran through Derrick's words again. "What do you mean, I'm going to have to pay?"

"We're not on video now," Derrick said through gritted teeth. "I switched to the loop I use when you sleep. I can do whatever I want to you, and there won't be any record. So you need to tell me what the message to Bridget really said. She hasn't figured it out yet, but I'm guessing she will, because she's smart. Like I know those names aren't actually characters in the books, so they must be a code. What did it say?"

"You're wrong, Derrick. They're real people." Bob pointed at the page, forgetting for a moment that Derrick was correct. "I'm writing about Ken and Jade right now. Look." He pulled the sheet of paper free, then handed it over. "And it's good. I'm really getting in the groove."

With a smirk, Derrick looked down. But when he looked up a minute later, the anger was gone. "What happens next?"

"I don't actually know. I have to write it. I can't figure out the book by talking about it. I have to think through my fingers."

After a moment, Derrick nodded, his earlier anger

forgotten. "I'll post this as a new sample. Once people see it, we'll sell a bunch more."

A woman's voice interrupted them. "What are you doing?"

They both startled and turned to the doorway. Joanne was standing with her hands on her hips.

"Mom? Why are you here?"

"I started driving as soon as those kids left. I realized I can't trust either one of you to do this right. In fact, before I came inside, I checked the Haldon Cam. So why did I just see a video of him walking on the treadmill, and even that's not true? We've got more than two dozen requests." Her grin was mercenary. "He might as well be making us some money."

"But he's writing, Mom. And it's really good."

"Like you're any judge of what's good or bad," Joanne scoffed. "You've gotten too close to him, Derrick. You need to get out of this room and clear your head." She bared her teeth at Bob in the nightmare version of a smile. "And I'll put him to work."

BRIDGET

Alphabet Soup

Bridget woke up late. For a second, she only knew something was wrong, but not what it was. Then she remembered. She pulled the pillow over her face and hid from the world.

The police and his assistant were convinced there was nothing wrong with Bob. They all thought she was just some obsessed fan.

Even Ajay.

She moved the pillow down, clutching it to her chest. She might be the only person in the world who knew Bob well enough to know something truly was wrong.

If she was right, the fate of the most famous fantasy writer in the world now rested in the hands of a seventeen-year-old girl.

Bridget picked up her laptop. The only thing she could think to do was to scour Bob's email again for clues.

She clicked on her inbox. Her heart sped up. There was a new email from Bob.

Hey Bridget—
Please ignore my previous message. I'm traveling

in Europe for research and the eight-hour time difference has really messed me up. As a result, I've been awake when I should be asleep and vice versa. Before I sent you my last email, I took an Ambien. When that didn't work, I was so desperate to sleep I took another one. And then I finally broke down and had a couple of those little vodka bottles from the hotel mini-fridge.

And all those things together finally worked. A little too well, as you already know. I had no idea I had written you until I got your concerned reply. Sorry for confusing you. That email even confuses me!

I'll be back in touch soon with some clearer questions. But until then, you don't need to worry.

Have a great Christmas,

Bob

Bridget knew she should sigh with relief. Instead, she heard herself say, "Huh."

On the surface, Bob's explanation made sense. He raised all the points Joanne and Ajay had.

But to Bridget, the second email seemed as stilted as the earlier one. Both felt wrong, just in different ways. In the first, he'd called her parents by the wrong names. And in the second, after supposedly sobering up, Bob didn't say one word about that. Didn't apologize for speaking about her mother as if she were still alive. And while Bob was gruff, and lived in his own little world, Bridget thought even he would have known how much pain his mistake would cause her. But he didn't mention it at all.

Was Bob really even in Flanders? All he said in the email was Europe. Had Joanne lied to them? Or had Bob lied to Joanne? And how could Bridget figure out the truth?

And then it came to her. Reddit. Even as someone who only visited the internet for research, she knew that one of the most popular subreddits was devoted to Swords and Shadows. But what she found on r/swordsandshadows left Bridget both more confused and more certain than ever.

A user named Rickard claimed chapters of *Eyes of the Forest* were being posted on the dark web and encouraged people to check them out. Was that even legal? Wouldn't Bob's publisher mind? Although if it was the dark web, maybe they didn't even know. And why would anyone pay a hundred dollars a chapter?

Only it sounded like some superfans had. She kept scrolling. The upvoted replies all agreed they really were written by Bob.

Bridget kept going deeper and deeper down Reddit holes. As she traced discussion threads that started at the level of trivia and then descended into minutiae, she was reminded why she normally avoided it. She was ready to stop when she stumbled over an obscure thread about something called the Haldon Cam. An icy finger traced her spine. Some people claimed that via the cam they had watched Bob type chapters.

It couldn't be real, could it? It didn't sound like many other people believed it. She kept scrolling through the replies. Toward the bottom of the thread, she saw something that froze her blood. A screenshot.

She squinted at the tiny image. Blurry, shot from overhead, it showed an older man in a half squat, his thumbs tucked in his armpits. His head was tilted down, so most of his face wasn't visible, just his thinning shaggy hair and a scruffy beard.

She enlarged the image. It did sort of look like him, if he'd stopped shaving and getting his hair cut. But the real Bob was rounder. And why would he ever squat like that? He certainly wasn't writing.

And if Bridget only half-believed it was Bob, the police never would. She went back to Bob's original email and read it again. And again. And again.

Hello Bridget—
You'll be glad to know I've turned my attention back to the manuscript and am making good progress. Have you had a chance to ask your parents about working for me full-time over the summer? Please tell Anna and Graham how much I'll need your help if I'm to finish.

As we discussed earlier, I'm adding a new character. So please look for all instances of:
"Jade Tarnno."

And then flag each spot with:
"Add Ken Pipem."

Suddenly it clicked.

Her parents weren't named Anna and Graham, but Bob hadn't made a mistake. He'd made a clue.

Anna and Graham. Anna Graham. Anagram.

Bob had been trying to tell her his email was really an anagram.

That still didn't solve the puzzle. His email had almost two hundred words. There must be thousands of potential combinations of words from those original dozens. It was like handing someone a tureen of alphabet soup and telling them *Romeo and Juliet* was in there if they just put all the letters in the right order.

On her next read through, Bridget zeroed in on the colons and the quotes. Bob never used colons like that. It seemed clunky. And the quotes were extraneous. Even though she hadn't previously articulated it to herself, the odd punctuation was part of the reason something had felt wrong. Could *Jade Tarnno* and *add Ken Pipem* be anagrams?

She started to write down the letters, then thought of an easier way. From the hall closet, she retrieved the worn Scrabble box.

After turning the tiles faceup on the dining room table, she plucked out the letters that spelled out *Jade Tarnno*. For an hour, she rearranged them, writing down possible combinations in her notebook.

Ajar Tendon
Ad Jan Toner
Dean Jar Ton
Dear Jan Not
Trade Jan On
And Roan Jet

It all looked like nonsense. Maybe she was on the wrong track. Maybe Bob had truly forgotten her parents' names.

She pushed the letters back into the center, and picked out the ones that spelled *add Ken Pipem*. Once again, she created a long list, mostly a random series of short words.

But there was at least one possible long word. She sucked in a breath.

Kidnap.

That still left a *d*, a *p*, two *e*'s, and an *m*. She swapped the remaining tiles back and forth until finally she had a phrase.

Kidnapped me.

She again selected the letters that made up *Jade Tarnno*. The *J* in *Jade* made her think of something. Someone. Already guessing the answer, she pulled out the letters that spelled out *Joanne*. That left her with *d-t-a-r*. Which could be rearranged to spell *Dart*. Joanne Dart.

And wasn't that what Officer Rubio had called her? Ms. Dart?

So together the two phrases read *Joanne Dart kidnapped me.*

Bridget's breath went shallow. Should she go to the

police? But she could already imagine their skepticism. Besides, she'd only solved part of his email. There had to be more information hidden in the rest. She kept reading it over until finally she saw it. The clue was hiding in plain sight. It started with the next sentence: *The rest of this letter details what I'm trying to get right on my third attempt, at least initially.*

There was no way Bob was working on a third draft. If he was, his queries would have become more frequent, but instead they had dwindled to nothing.

She focused on the sentence's last clause . . . *at least initially.* Was she supposed to look at the first letter of each word?

Bridget picked up her pen.

c y h w r e c y l u w d c b i o t n c t m w i t l t h a p o w n o f a d b a c b o a s w b t m i w p n s m h w a e c t l j k p

She could see words like *wit, own, fad* and *boas,* but they seemed random, coincidences in a string of nonsense.

Third attempt. Maybe she was supposed to look at the first letter of every third word? Within a few seconds, it was clear that was the solution.

And finally Bridget had the whole thing. The second reassuring email must have been false, written under duress. Or perhaps written by someone else entirely. Horror washed over her as she reread Bob's last true message.

Joanne Dart kidnapped me. Held in Mt. Hood cabin. Help.

Then Bridget had all but told Joanne that Bob was trying to fool her.

So what had Joanne done next?

BRIDGET

Safety Depends on You

Bridget tried to slow down her breathing. Bob was being held in a cabin on Mount Hood. There must be dozens, if not hundreds, of such cabins. On her own, there was no way she could figure out where he was. Even if she could, what could she do?

She had to go to the police. Now that she had proof of Bob's secret message, they would have to listen to her. They would arrest Joanne and force her to reveal where she was keeping Bob.

As she got dressed, Bridget debated whether to tell Ajay, who by now would be on his way to Seattle. She was still hurt he hadn't believed her, but he also deserved to know the truth. It was too complicated to explain in a text, so she put it in an email. Writing it all out helped organize her thoughts.

After she hit the SEND key, she set out for the small-town police station closest to Bob's house. Driving in silence except for the occasional direction from Google Maps, she rehearsed what she would say.

The police department was housed in a one-story

redbrick building. Bridget's breathing went shallow as she walked in. The lobby held a few chairs, a fake plant, and a large rack of brochures. The room was cut in half by a counter topped with thick glass. Behind it two people in street clothes were working at metal desks. The younger African American guy was on the phone. The older white woman looked up from her computer. When she saw Bridget, she stood and walked up to the counter. She pressed a button, and her tinny voice issued from an intercom overhead.

"Can I help you?"

"I need to speak to an officer." Bridget wiped her sweaty palms on her pants.

"What about?"

"I want to report a kidnapping."

The woman's gaze sharpened. "Who's been kidnapped?"

"B—I mean, R. M. Haldon."

Her brows drew together. "The author?"

Bridget nodded.

After a pause, the clerk said, "All our officers are on patrol, but I'll have dispatch send one back here. What's your name?"

"Bridget. Bridget Shepherd."

"Okay, Bridget. Have a seat. We'll have an officer here in about ten minutes to talk to you."

But Bridget couldn't sit. She went over to the wall of brochures. Just running her gaze over the titles heightened her anxiety.

HOME ALONE: A PARENT'S GUIDE

BEING FORCED INTO HAVING SEX IS RAPE AND IT'S A CRIME

FIREARMS SAFETY DEPENDS ON YOU

ONLINE ALONE: INTERNET SAFETY TIPS FOR KIDS

DON'T BE THE VICTIM OF A SCAMMER

DATING VIOLENCE: IS IT ABUSE?

WOULD YOUR CHILD KNOW WHAT TO DO?

IF A POLICE OFFICER STOPS YOUR VEHICLE

"Bridget?" a man said behind her.

With a start, she turned to face an Asian guy who didn't look much older than her. "Yeah?"

"I'm Samuel Poon." He held out his hand. His head was faintly shadowed where the hair had been shaved off. Maybe he'd been going for tough, but instead it made him look vulnerable, like a baby bird.

Her carefully crafted explanation flew out of her head. "I'm here because Bob—R. M. Haldon—has been kidnapped. He tried to send me a message, but I didn't understand it at first. Then I figured it out, and now I'm afraid something even worse has happened to him."

His brows rose. "I want to help you, but first why don't we go back and sit down. Then you can explain to me what's happening."

"Okay."

He waved his keycard over a sensor. A door into the glassed-in area opened. They walked past the two clerks, both now on the phone.

Officer Poon ushered Bridget inside a small, plain

room that held two chairs and a table. He left the door open.

"So you were saying something about how R. M. Haldon has been kidnapped?" From his chest pocket, he pulled out a little notebook and flipped it open, clicked his pen.

Bridget took out her phone. "Look. It started when he sent me this email. I knew something was wrong with it, but it took me a while to figure out it's all in code."

"In code," he repeated. He set down his notebook and took her phone. As he scrolled down, his brow furrowed.

"But I finally unscrambled it." And it all came tumbling out—her work on the database, her parents' real names and the names Bob had used, what she'd seen on Reddit, and finally how she'd figured out the clues and solved the true meaning hidden in Bob's message.

Officer Poon twisted his head as if he was having trouble hearing her. "So all that is why you think Mr. Haldon's been kidnapped."

"Yes!" Bridget was relieved someone was finally listening to her. "Like he says in the hidden message, he was kidnapped by his assistant. That Joanne Dart woman. Or"—the thought suddenly struck her—"I don't know, maybe she just says she's his assistant but she's not really."

Officer Poon exhaled heavily. "Ms. Dart actually *is* his housekeeper. I've dealt with her several times."

"Oh." Bridget recalculated. "Okay. Well, I guess that makes sense. If she works for him, it would be easy for her to kidnap him."

"And now you say she's selling chapters of Mr. Haldon's new book on the dark web? Have you seen this yourself?"

"I don't even know how to go on there," Bridget admitted. "It didn't seem safe to look for it myself."

He pressed his lips together. "Then how do you know that's what's happening?"

"I told you. I saw it on Reddit." She took the phone back, went to the site, and started clicking and scrolling. "And then I saw this photo. I'm almost certain that's Bob, only he's thinner for some reason." Tears pricked her eyes. "It sounds like they might be making him do tricks for money."

She held the phone out, but instead of taking it, he said, "Let me ask you something, Bridget. Do you think people are following you?"

What was Officer Poon saying? Had he seen something suspicious out in the parking lot? She hadn't paid much attention on the drive over. "I guess they could be?"

"Hm." He nodded, as if deciding something. "Are you under a doctor's care? Is there someone I can call to be with you?"

The truth crashed down on her. "You don't believe me."

"Look—I believe *you* believe it."

She got to her feet. "But Bob's really in trouble! You have to believe me."

Raising his open hands, he patted the air. "Calm down. I'm here to help you."

"I don't need help. It's *Bob* that needs help."

And suddenly Bridget saw herself as Officer Poon must. She had become a living version of the meme from in *It's Always Sunny in Philadelphia*, the one where a paranoid Charlie covered the wall with layers of printouts and photos, and drew a web of incomprehensible connections between them while ranting about conspiracies.

Officer Poon was probably waiting for Bridget to declare the CIA was controlling her mind, or that she was an angel of the Lord.

And then things got even worse. Bridget saw movement out of the corner of one eye. When she turned, she saw Officer Rubio, with her hands on her hips.

"What's the topic of discussion? It wouldn't be Mr. Haldon by any chance, would it?"

"Miss Shepherd has a very complicated story," Officer Poon said, his voice sliding on the word *complicated*. "I was just asking her if she was on any medication."

"Which I am *not*!" Bridget crossed her arms.

"Sam, I dealt with Miss Shepherd yesterday, and I don't share your concerns. She's just a very big fan, one who's maybe gotten in a little too deep. As I told her yesterday, Mr. Haldon is an adult. He's allowed to leave town or even the country whenever he wants. He doesn't have to tell anyone—including his fans—where he's going, whether that's Europe for research or just down the street for coffee. And as you learned yesterday, Bridget, Ms. Dart's been in touch with him."

"Been in touch with him! She kidnapped him!"

Officer Rubio inhaled sharply. "Look, do you know how many times we have been called to his house to deal with a fan claiming she's married to him, or that they're really his daughter or son, or the mother of his child? Or they think he really is King Travis or whoever that guy is?"

Bridget started to protest, but Officer Rubio overrode her. "Listen to me. You need to get a life. You need to pull yourself together and snap out of it. You've been watching too many movies, playing too many video games. Those fantasy books may be full of excitement and convoluted plots, but this is real life, which, frankly, is pretty boring."

Bridget resisted the urge to stamp her foot. "But I'm telling the truth. Bob's been kidnapped. Or why else would he send me a coded message?"

Officer Rubio made an impatient noise. "I'm not going to get deep in the weeds here. Maybe one of your friends is pranking you. All I know is you're taking this way too personally. Go talk about it at your Comic Con or your fan club or whatever. But you have to stop wasting our time when we've got more than enough real problems to deal with."

BOB

An Odd, Defiant Joy

In the darkest cell, deep under the castle, Ken Pipem was singing. He sang of ancient kings who had gladly laid down their lives for their men. Of the noble unicorns. Of the magical mirror that could both save and destroy. Of betrayal and murder and sacrifice. He sang of Skin Changers and hanged men, of endless love and eternal longing. His voice was full of pain and bravery and an odd, defiant joy.

Sitting in her own cell, Jancy thought Ken's song was the most beautiful thing she had ever heard. It was a golden thread lacing together the patchwork of centuries, scraps of tales old and new, turning them into a tapestry of history. For a moment, Jancy saw she was just one small knot in a larger work.

She tipped her head back against the cold wall of her cell, the limestone damp against her scalp. She considered trying to lick the moisture from the walls. She had had naught to drink for two days, and her tongue was a piece of leather in her mouth.

How was Ken even managing to sing? Had a guard
given him a furtive sip?

Still, she could not begrudge it, because his strong,
sweet voice offered the only respite from her thoughts.

Tomorrow, both she and Ken would die.

"Bob!" Derrick said from the doorway. "Earth to Bob!
Come in!"

Bob lifted his hands from the keys. Slowly, the room
came back into focus. The rough stone walls became
smooth yellow pine. The sounds of Ken singing were
replaced by the hum of the treadmill, the soft thud of his
footfalls.

And by the sound of Derrick's slightly nasal voice.
"Already up and at 'em, huh? It's your lucky day. You get
a shower."

Bob hit the stop button on the treadmill. He must
have typed all night. His body might be in this room, but
his mind was still in the world of *Eyes of the Forest*.

What would happen next? He could almost feel it.
Almost see it, but it was as if he was peering through fog
on a dark night. Ken would die, Bob knew that much, but
not by the headsman's axe. The truth of King Tristan's
murder would be revealed. Orwen, now King Orwen,
would battle Rowan, the peasant rebellion's leader. The
battle would be infinitely complicated by the arrival of
the Armies of the Night, which threatened to wipe out
all humankind. The unicorns might ally themselves with
humans or follow their own self-interests. And Jancy
would finally have to choose between Orwen and Rowan—or would she? Suddenly Bob wasn't quite sure.

Derrick was unlocking the shackles from the cable. Slowly Bob became aware of how his ankles were throbbing, rubbed raw despite new socks.

"Come on." Derrick straightened up. After the shower, Bob would ask to wear two pairs of socks. Maybe request some sort of padding. But even if the boy denied him everything, it would still be a joy to climb back up on the treadmill, to put his fingers to the keys, and to let the story unfurl.

Somehow Bob had become Ken Pipem, singing despite captivity and the threat of death, weaving a story despite—or perhaps because of—the all-enveloping darkness.

BRIDGET

Compact and Discreet

It was up to her now, Bridget thought, driving home from the police station. First she had to figure out where Bob was, and then she had to rescue him. It seemed impossible. But she had to try.

Once home, she went straight to her computer and typed in *Joanne Dart* and *Mt. Hood*, both in quotes. Nothing. She tried substituting *cabin* for *Mt. Hood*. Still nothing. There must be property records someplace, but she had no idea how to access them, or if it was possible to start with the owner's name and then work back to the address. And who knew if Joanne even owned the cabin? It could belong to a friend or family member. It could even be that she was taking advantage of a cabin only used in the summer.

Maybe Bridget could follow Joanne until she returned to wherever she was holding Bob.

Bridget put her fingers back on the keyboard. But now she substituted *address* for *cabin*. This time she got results. She clicked the top link.

We found 6 records in 6 states for Joanne Dart in the US. The top state of residence is California, followed by Arizona. The average Joanne Dart falls into the age group of 61–80.

And there on the list of names and addresses was Bob's Joanne Dart, a veritable youngster compared to her peers. Joanne Dart, 48, 2377 SW Winding Road Way, Portland, Oregon. Next to Joanne's name was a button Bridget could click to purchase more information, including email addresses, social media profiles, and criminal records.

But what Bridget needed—Joanne's full home address—was right there on the main, free listing. Bridget could stake it out, wait for her to leave, and then follow her Honda.

Reality set in. From watching cop shows, Bridget knew that when the police followed a suspect, they used several vehicles and took turns so the suspect didn't get suspicious. Even though a Subaru Outback was Portland's unofficial car, it seemed likely Joanne would eventually notice Bridget driving behind her, especially on rural roads.

In the Google search bar, Bridget typed in *How to secretly follow someone.*

A few clicks later, she was on an Amazon product page.

Peace of mind comes from knowing where everything is at all times. Do you need an easy yet stealthy way to track a teenager's vehicle, a possibly philandering spouse, a wandering pet, an elderly parent, luggage, or other important belongings? Compact and discreet, our tracker is easy to slip into a backpack or piece of luggage. Or use its built-in magnet to attach it to the underside of a vehicle. Then our easy-to-use app will let you remotely track movements in real-time.

Just reading the product description made Bridget feel dirty. Since when were people "important belongings"?

Then she clicked the BUY button and paid extra for one-day delivery.

Next she drove to Joanne's house to scope out the situation. It was in a newer clutch of houses, a neighborhood with cul-de-sacs and sidewalks. The houses were all variations on the same theme, two stories tall, painted in neutral colors, with closed two-car garages. This last observation made Bridget bite her lip. There would be no attaching the magnet in the middle of the night if the car was inside the garage.

But Joanne's black Honda was sitting in the driveway. Bridget didn't vary her speed or even turn her head as she drove past. A few blocks away, she found a spot on the edge of a small park where she could park the car when she returned with the tracker.

What else did she need? At Dick's Sporting Goods, she picked up a pair of binoculars. Once she confirmed Bob was being held captive, she'd call the local police. In case she was confronted, she also got a baseball bat. Her last purchase was a Leatherman tool. If she had to, she could unscrew a door hinge or saw through ropes.

The tracker arrived the next morning. Bridget spent most of the day in her garage, figuring out the fastest way to slap on the magnet. When night fell, she dressed in head-to-toe black, like a pedestrian with a death wish. She even put on Ajay's socks, which were surprisingly thick and warm. For a few hours, she dozed on the couch, dreaming terrible dreams of hitting Joanne in the head with the bat, or even worse, of Joanne shooting her.

Finally, at two in the morning, Bridget got up, put on

her black coat and gloves, and pulled a black neck gaiter over the lower part of her face and a black beanie over her hair.

After parking in the spot she'd picked out, she got out and immediately started to shiver. The forecasters were talking about snow, and she could feel it in the heavy stillness. The air was so cold each breath seemed to pull her lungs inside out. By the time she reached Joanne's block, Bridget was shaking so hard she was afraid she'd drop the tracker. No matter how lightly she tried to walk, each footstep echoed hollowly. She kept waiting for a dog to bark, a light to blink on.

But the world around her remained dark and hushed. And finally she was on Joanne's block, and then just a few feet from her car.

Hunched over, Bridget scuttled over to the driver's side door, which was the furthest from the house. Just as she'd practiced on her dad's car, she slapped the magnet underneath the door frame. And then she was gone. She ran the last two blocks to her dad's car.

Back home, Bridget couldn't sleep. Ajay hadn't answered her email. Nobody knew what she was planning to do. At best, Ajay thought she was mentally ill and the police thought she was an obsessed loser. But in her heart she knew she was Bob's only chance.

At four A.M., when she still couldn't sleep, she pulled her laptop onto her bed and wrote Ajay another email, telling him what she was planning on doing and giving him instructions on how to use the tracker. Would he just shake his head, chalk it up to more proof she'd fallen down the rabbit hole, and then hit the DELETE key?

Finally, she was able to sleep. When she woke up, the light in the room told her it was late morning. Before getting out of bed, she went to the tracking page.

Joanne was already on the move. Bridget's heart kicked in her chest. Should she run to her car, start following now? But, she reminded herself, that was what the tracker was for.

Five minutes later, the dot was stationary. It was still in Portland. In fact, when she zoomed in on the map, Bridget knew exactly where Bob's assistant was. Not at a Mount Hood cabin.

She was at Costco.

Bridget groaned. *Costco.* She hoped Ajay hadn't picked this time to check out the tracker.

After a shower, she made herself an oversized mug of coffee. She had a second one with her cereal and started to feel slightly human. She toggled back and forth between her email—nothing from Ajay—and the tracker—Joanne was still at Costco. Probably picking up cleaning supplies to give Bob's house a really thorough going-over while he was in Flanders.

But then the dot started to move. First it was on Interstate 5, then Interstate 84. And when it turned onto Highway 26, Bridget was sure she knew where it was going. Highway 26 was the road to Mount Hood.

The dot kept moving until finally, after about forty-five minutes, it came to a stop on a street called Hoot Owl Road. Somewhere near the Zigzag River, but several miles from even the smallest town.

Someplace isolated. A perfect place to hold someone hostage.

Bridget waited until midafternoon to see if Joanne left. But the dot stayed put. She had to leave now if she didn't want to drive in the dark. She put on heavy winter clothes, and waterproof hiking boots. The Leatherman went in her pocket, and the bat and binoculars on the car's passenger seat.

As she turned onto Highway 26, it was starting to snow, fat white flakes that seemed to suck up all the sound. By the time she turned onto Hoot Owl Road, still three miles from her destination, the snow was coming faster, the flakes smaller, and night was coming on. She turned the wipers up another notch, leaning forward and squinting. Even though Bridget was going so slow the speedometer barely registered, she could not see more than a few feet in front of her. The snow felt like a blanket that had been draped over the car, pressing up against the windows, isolating her.

The rear tires fishtailed. Her heart stuttered even as they found purchase. Should she shift the car into a lower gear? Bridget had never driven on snow before. With a start, she realized she'd gotten closer to the cabin than she intended. She had planned to stop well short and approach on foot, but suddenly it was right there, a faint glow in the dark to her left.

And just as she was thinking that, the car suddenly jolted as it hit something.

DERRICK

Save Him

In Portland, Derrick wouldn't have paid any attention to the sound of an approaching car. Not even in Cascadia, where a real road ran next to the imaginary battlefield. But in the dead silence of the forest, he and his mom could hear the engine's low grumble long before they saw it.

"Who do you think it is?" he asked as they both peered out the living room window, trying to see through the snow.

"I don't think it's the cops." His mom bit her lip. "But there's also no way anyone could come down our road by accident, especially not in this weather. So it must have something to do with Bob."

They both squinted through the glass. Finally, Derrick was able to make out a dark-colored car. Joanne hissed, and he turned to look at her.

"It's that Bridget girl. His researcher." She pressed her nose against the window. "But this time she's alone."

Derrick jumped when a loud thump suddenly shook the house. It sounded like someone had just pushed a couch out a second-story window. Shock turned to anger when he realized the sound had really been Bridget's car hitting his Toyota.

It was all spiraling out of control. He threw on his coat. "You stay with Bob and keep him quiet. I'll go out and see what's going on." He grabbed the airsoft gun from the end table and stuffed it into his pocket.

When he ran out, Bridget was just getting out of her car. The impact had been at an angle, damaging one corner of his rear bumper and one corner of her front bumper.

"You just hit my car!" The pain in his voice was no act. He'd traded a lot of Cascadia coin for real dollars to buy the car off Craigslist. Even if he could now afford to buy a half-dozen replacements, that didn't mean he didn't still love his old car.

"I'm sorry!" She was visibly shaking. "I got lost, and I couldn't see through the snow. I didn't see your car. I couldn't even see the road." Her voice changed. "Derrick? What are you doing here?"

He found the answer even as he said it. "Are you here for R. M. Haldon too?"

"Yes." Bridget drew out the word hesitantly.

"I just got here myself. I love his books so much. I even play the character based on Rowan in Mysts of Cascadia, this LARP—live-action role play. And then when I saw him online, I was so sure I was going to save him." To Derrick's ears, his laugh sounded real and genuinely bitter. "You can imagine how stupid I felt once I realized it was all Haldon's—I mean Bob's—idea."

It was just like LARPing. Spinning a tale that incorporated the major plot points while glossing over the bits that didn't quite fit.

"What?" Bridget's mouth fell open.

"Here, come up on the porch out of the snow." He started up the stairs, and she followed. Through the windows, he saw his mother was no longer in the living room. Derrick turned to face Bridget. "Bob told me he holed up in this cabin so he could write. He said he needed to be away from all distractions, all his toys." His words sounded true because they were.

Bridget looked at the Honda. "Is that why his assistant's car is here?"

"Uh-huh. She just brought him supplies from Costco. And she's under strict orders not to reveal the truth."

"But he sent me a message that Joanne kidnapped him."

"Really?" He feigned confusion. "That can't be right. He was just complaining to her that she didn't bring him any junk food. He's not acting like she's a kidnapper. And she seems pretty normal to me. Other than being really sick of fanboys. That's what she was calling me until Bob made her stop."

Bridget's nose scrunched up in an appealing way. "But on Reddit they're saying someone on the dark web is selling chapters of *Eyes of the Forest*. Even selling the ability to order Bob to do things on camera."

Derrick shrugged, glad the curtains to Bob's room were closed. "That's why I'm here. I got worried about him. But it turns out that's all coming straight from Bob. He's just pretending to be kidnapped. He says the accountability of people expecting regular chapters is keeping him honest. And the requests for tricks amuse him. He likes to see what people think up."

"Really?"

"He even let me read a little bit of the new stuff he's writing to thank me for coming all the way out here. Do you want to come in and talk to him?"

Bridget looked relieved. "Of course."

He put his hand on the doorknob and turned to her with a smile. "I'm just glad I didn't tell anyone what I was doing before I came here. Can you imagine how stupid I'd look once they knew the truth?" He leaned in, his voice conspiratorial. "I hope you didn't tell anyone."

BRIDGET

How Much Worse Could It Get?

So you're sure they can't hear us?" Bridget whispered to Bob. They were both sitting on the edge of his unmade bed. Her head was turned so her lips were hidden from the camera. She was trembling, still feeling the aftershocks of the fender bender and its aftermath.

After she'd stupidly said no one knew she was coming here (since Ajay either didn't know or didn't care), Derrick had pulled a gun on her. Derrick, Joanne's son.

He was Joanne's son.

Derrick had forced her inside, where Joanne conducted a thorough and impersonal search, confiscating Bridget's car keys and the Leatherman tool. Her phone and the baseball bat were still in the car. Then they'd brought her into this room and undone one of Bob's shackles. Before leaving them, Derrick had shackled Bridget's left leg to Bob's right, which was also attached by a cable to the treadmill desk. He'd even taken her boots.

At first Bridget had wondered if their prisoner even *was* Bob. Not just because of the longish hair and scruffy beard, but because this man was maybe three-fourths the size of the Bob she remembered. But as Derrick closed the cuff around her ankle, Bob had given her a small, sad smile that pierced her heart. It was the same look he'd given her when he learned about her mother's death.

For the last half hour, they had been whispering, catching each other up on what had happened. Bob had covered his face with his hands when he admitted the kidnapping had originally been his idea, and then explained, with an out-of-place joy, that he had finally broken through his writer's block. Bridget had told him about the cops' jaded reaction. The whole time they had been talking, Joanne and Derrick had been too, out in the living room. Arguing, by the sound of it, although Bridget couldn't make out the words.

Bob pointed out the camera to her. "I'm pretty sure whoever is watching can't hear us. Derrick usually turns the sound off unless they've gotten a request for me to say something."

"He was asking these weird questions about you back on Halloween. I think he must have figured out I was your researcher. Everyone at school knows he's a total fanboy of yours. And of course he would cast himself as the Rowan character."

"Nobody wants to be third spear carrier from the left," Bob said mildly.

"You're acting pretty calm for someone who's being held hostage."

"I've had a lot of time to get used to it. And Derrick's not a bad kid. His mom is the one who scares me. She's a little trigger happy with that stun gun. But now that you're here, I'm worried they'll decide to use you as a bargaining chip. One they don't care about but know I do." He flushed and looked away. "Speaking of which, I'm sorry I had to mention your mom in that note. I was just trying to figure out how to get your attention."

Bridget sighed. "That's okay. And I apologize for how long it took me to understand what was really going on. I only checked on the Swords and Shadows Reddit a couple of days ago. A few people have seen your video on the dark web, but most don't think it's real. Especially once you started doing tricks for money."

He grimaced. "That was Joanne's idea."

"Most people seem to have decided you're just some weird guy who looks a little like you. You know, they think this whole thing is a novelty act, one of the internet's weird corners. But I think if we could make your fans realize it *is* real, we could get them to call the police."

"How are we going to do that? Even when the sound's on, either Joanne or Derrick is always hovering right outside the frame."

She straightened up. "We could hold up a sign asking for help. I don't know the exact address of this place, just that it's three miles once you turn on Hoot Owl Road."

Bob sighed. "The only thing I have to write with is the typewriter, but the type is too small for them to read. Derrick could only see I was typing, not what it said."

"What about if you got on top of that desk and held a note a few inches away from the cam?"

He looked skeptical. "How's that going to work? We're chained together, and there's not room on top of that desk for both of us."

Bridget measured distances with her eyes. "I think if I lay on my back on the treadmill and stuck my legs straight up, there would be enough slack in the chain for you to get on the desk."

Bob shook his head. "I'm not getting up there. It's not safe."

The actual danger was waiting for Joanne and Derrick to decide what to do with them. "Okay, then you lie on your back, and I'll climb up."

He pressed his lips together. "What if they come in and catch us?"

"Do you think they're really going to let us go? Besides, how much worse could it get?"

Outside, the wind was howling. Bob shivered. "Maybe quite a lot, especially for you. They won't kill me while I'm still writing the book. It's why I've made sure to never finish. At least not the book Derrick is reading."

"I think I have to try." As Bridget was speaking, the lights flickered. "And I'd better hurry in case the power goes out."

"The camera runs on cellular service, so as long as the towers are okay, it should work."

"But if it's dark, no one will be able to see anything," Bridget pointed out.

"We just better hope that Derrick doesn't think to switch the camera over. When I'm supposed to be asleep, he loops the day's footage so it looks like I'm always writing." Bob snorted softly. "I guess the joke's on him, because it's true."

Together, they moved to the desk. It was awkward moving in tandem, like the world's worst sack race. Bob had to roll the paper into the typewriter, because Bridget didn't know how, but she did the typing with the CAPS LOCK key on. It was weird how far her fingers had to travel and how hard they had to strike, but also oddly thrilling to see the words appear letter by letter.

HELP!!! CALL POLICE. R. M. HALDON, AUTHOR OF SWORDS AND SHADOWS, AND BRIDGET SHEPHERD HAVE BEEN KIDNAPPED BY HIS ASSISTANT JOANNE DART. HELD HOSTAGE IN MT HOOD CABIN ON HOOT OWL ROAD.

"Three exclamation points." He raised one bushy eyebrow as he freed the paper and handed it over. "Don't you find that a bit excessive?"

"Not when it's life or death." She pushed the typewriter aside. "Now you get down, and I'll get up.

With a muffled groan, Bob lay on his back on the treadmill, curling his knees to his chest. He wiggled until his butt was even with the desk's front edge, then straightened his legs. She braced her hands on the work surface. Jumping up, she got one knee on and then the other. Moving carefully, she stood up as Bob straightened his legs.

Every move was foreshortened with a bruising yank on both their legs.

Bridget picked up the paper. Holding her arms overhead, she held the sign as close to the camera as she could. She slowly counted to fifteen, then pulled it back a few inches in case it was too close and cutting off a key phrase. Another count of fifteen, and she held it against her chest. Then she repeated the sequence.

She tried to imagine what was happening on the other end of the broadcast. Were viewers googling Joanne Dart? Checking Google Maps for Hoot Owl Road? Or laughing at what was apparently a weird joke? Maybe no one was looking at her note at all. Or maybe the cam wasn't even working because Derrick had set it to broadcast one of those loops Bob had talked about. She just hoped Derrick was distracted by the argument with his mom, which, judging by the yelling, was still going on.

Her thoughts were interrupted by Bob loudly clearing his throat. She looked down. He was frantically gesturing for her to get off the desk. Someone must be coming.

Bridget started to kneel. But if they saw the typewriter pushed to one side, it would be a big clue as to what they had been doing. She leaned over and began to move it back into place. But as she did, she lost her balance. Suddenly she was tumbling off the desktop.

For a second, she had the illusion she might catch herself. Then her right shoulder slammed into the floor. At the same time, her legs pinwheeled overhead, until the chain abruptly jerked her left leg back. Pulled in two directions, Bridget felt like a turkey wishbone at Thanksgiving. When she finally stopped, she was lying on her right side facing away from the treadmill, while her left leg was straight up and nearly behind her.

Somehow Bridget had managed not to scream at the shock and pain. Not that it mattered, because Bob had shouted. And her fall had been so noisy.

Any second they would come in here and discover the sign. With her last bit of effort, she slid the paper under the treadmill. As she did, she saw short stacks of pages already hidden underneath.

With a wince, she probed her shoulder and then her ankle as she turned toward Bob. She was going to have some horrible bruises, but nothing was out of place. Nothing was broken.

And then she saw Bob's right foot. It was bent at an odd angle, dangling like a half-kicked-off shoe.

The room went dark.

DERRICK

So Wrong, So Fast

Derrick was running to Bob's room to see what had caused the loud crash when the power went out. With a thumb, he swiped the flashlight setting on his phone as he threw open the door. He half expected to see a broken window and an empty room.

Bridget and Bob were both still there, but something was broken, all right.

Bob's right ankle. Dark blood on his dirty white sock and his foot at the wrong angle. Derrick's stomach somersaulted at the sight. It was disgusting. It took all of his willpower not to throw up, but to instead find the key and set it in the lock. He tried to unlatch the cuff without actually focusing on anything.

His mom added the light of her own phone. After coming in, she reached down and yanked off Bob's sock.

He screamed. Not only was there a bloody gash, but also something white and shiny. A bone, broken and now poking through the skin.

"What did you do, you stupid girl?" Joanne demanded.

"I tripped and fell." Bridget was on her knees next to Bob, who lay moaning on his back on the treadmill. Her face contorted. "I'm sorry."

After Derrick removed the cuff—the old man certainly wasn't going anyplace—he put it on her other leg so that she was wearing both halves of the shackles. When he looked back at the doorway, his mom had disappeared. Panic swept over him. He didn't know what to do.

But then she returned carrying a small red-and-white plastic bottle and a glass of water.

"Looks like these Tylenol are expired, but they're all we've got."

When Derrick tried to help him sit up, Bob went rigid and screamed. But finally they got him to swallow four pills. Bridget was crying softly.

His mom's upper lip curled in disgust as she played her phone's light over the wound. It wasn't bleeding as much as Derrick would have expected, but that was the only good thing about it.

"We're going to have to try to put the bone back in," she finally said. "You"—she pointed at Bridget—"clear off the bed so we can get him on it."

Bridget scrambled to pull back the covers, the chain between her cuffs jingling. Derrick and Joanne managed to get a moaning Bob up onto one foot, with his arms around their shoulders. Bob had to brace himself on them each time he swung his good foot forward. Even only taking half the weight, Derrick was glad the old man had lost a few pounds.

Bob finally fell more than sat on the bed, still holding his right leg suspended in the air. Groaning, he scooted back on his elbows until his knee was supported by the mattress, his leg jutting off it.

"All right, girl, you and I are going to have to hold on to his leg just below the knee." None-too-gently, Joanne tugged up the bottom cuff of Bob's sweatpants. After propping her phone on a pillow, she leaned over and put her hands on either side of his knee, just above the joint. She instructed Bridget to get on the other side and hold just below. "Okay, Derrick, now you take his foot in both hands, pull it back and try to straighten it out until the bone slips back in."

Derrick's vision went blurry. How had everything gone so wrong, so fast? "Can't you do it?" he protested.

"I don't know that this whole thing is such a good idea," Bob said urgently.

Joanne answered as if only Derrick had spoken. "You're stronger than I am."

Chewing his lip, he put his phone on the top of the treadmill desk, propping it against the typewriter. It didn't provide that much light, for which he was actually glad. Derrick tentatively laid one hand on the top of Bob's disgusting, bare, sweaty foot. It was hairy, which made it even grosser. He cupped his other hand around the callused heel.

"In fact, I think this is a really bad idea." Bob's tone was even more urgent.

"Be quiet," Joanne said. "And don't move." She took a deep breath. "Okay, on the count of three. One. Two. Three."

Derrick tightened his grip and started to pull the foot toward him, angling it a little bit.

Bob screamed, high and shrill. Suddenly, mercifully, he stopped. With a thump, he flopped back on the bed.

"Keep going!" Joanne ordered. "Finish it before he comes to."

Derrick pulled harder this time, trying to focus in the dim room on the dark splotch that marked where the bone had broken through the skin. Through his hands, he felt the vibration of something clicking back into place.

"That's it!" Joanne said. "Good job." Rare praise, but it barely registered.

When Derrick picked up his phone to check Bob's leg, the bone had disappeared.

But things did not actually look that much better. There was still a bloody gash. And the whole area was starting to look puffy.

Putting the bone back into place was just the start. They needed prescription pain medication, antibiotics, sterile conditions, and an orthopedic surgeon.

What they had was expired Tylenol and three people who had no idea what they were doing.

"Let's get him the right way on the bed," Derrick suggested.

Together the three of them maneuvered Bob into more or less the correct orientation. In a weird way, it felt like they were now co-conspirators. Even though Derrick and Joanne were the ones who had brought Bob here, it was Bridget who had broken his ankle. Now she lifted

Bob's head and put a pillow under it. She gently draped the covers over his torso.

"Do you have any ice we could put on his foot?" she asked.

Derrick gestured toward the window, feeling a harsh laugh bubble up. "Miles of it."

"I think we need to splint it first," Joanne said. "And it's probably better if we do it while he's still unconscious. Derrick, go get some of those old magazines from the living room. And then you can fill a garbage bag or two with snow."

The splint they made ended up looking totally ridiculous. They padded his ankle with washcloths and then tied two old copies of *National Geographic* around it with kitchen twine. After propping his leg up on an extra blanket from the hall cupboard, they put two garbage bags full of snow on either side.

After that, Derrick and Joanne left Bridget to watch Bob, and they went to bed.

But Derrick couldn't sleep, especially after Bob's moans started floating down the hall. His head felt full of static, and his body vibrated with itchy panic.

If Bob died, then he would never finish *Eyes of the Forest.*

AJAY

Mix of Feelings

Ajay sat in the back seat of the car, idly playing with his phone. Beside him, Aprita was asleep, a balled-up sweater serving as a cushion between her and the window. In the front seats, his parents were listening to NPR.

Outside, the traffic stopped and started for no reason that he could see. On paper, Portland and Seattle were three hours apart, but that was only true if there were no other cars on the road. Today, that certainly wasn't the case. And even though Portlanders complained about their traffic, Seattle's was even worse.

Over the past few days, Ajay had cooked a few dishes in his aunt's kitchen, patiently played board games with his cousins (all younger), and avoided Aprita's attempts to ask him about Bridget. How could he explain what was happening? He didn't know how to describe it to himself.

All the passion that had drawn him to Bridget had been revealed as something scarier, something that erased the boundary between imagination and reality. She had fallen so far into Swords and Shadows that she had decided to create a world where she herself was part of the books.

But thinking about Bridget made him feel anxious and sad. So now Ajay distracted himself by playing Candy Crush and Word Finder. He checked out the *Onion* and *Bored Panda*. Every now and then he would look up to see how much closer they were to Portland, and every time he was disappointed to realize how much longer it would be.

Finally, when he had exhausted every possible form of time waster, Ajay checked his Gmail account. Amid the junk mail were two personal emails. The sight of them made him feel the weirdest mix of feelings because of who they were from: Bridget Shepherd.

Already wincing, Ajay opened the first. It explained that she had discovered a code in "Bob's" message. Reading the first paragraph was enough to make him want to kick and shout, to try to do something to release his anger and frustration at how her mental illness still had her in its grasp. A code. Good grief. Pretty soon she would be telling him that strangers were following her and her phone was being tapped. He powered off the phone and tried to mimic Aprita and sleep.

But sleep wouldn't come. Ajay opened up her email again, read a little further. The police hadn't believed her, which was a relief.

But at the bottom of the email, when she told him how she had solved it, it almost made a kind of sense.

Right, Ajay reminded himself. Sense. There was no way Bob was being held captive. He was on the verge of becoming just as bad as Bridget. Bridget, who had probably made the entire message up anyway and sent it to herself.

And then Ajay read her second email. About the tracker she was applying to Joanne's car. Now Bridget's internal demons were being let out into the real world.

BRIDGET

Shadows of the Real

Despite Joanne coming in to give Bob four more Tylenol around midnight, he had whimpered and writhed all night. Bridget had finally fallen into something like sleep, curled up on the floor wrapped in a blanket. They had let her keep her coat. Every time she turned onto her bruised shoulder, the pain roused her.

In the morning, she woke to a hushed silence. *Oh, please God, no.* Her eyes flew open. The room was filled with a pearlescent light.

Bridget jolted up, pinning her eyes to Bob's gray face. Then he drew in a ragged breath and she could release her own. He was still alive, sleeping an uneasy sleep. Even though the room was so cold she could see her breath, Bob's face was shiny with sweat.

As quietly as possible, she got to her feet. Outside, the snow was falling steadily. But the power hadn't come back on. Looking out at the world blanketed in white, she hugged the blanket tighter around herself, and not just because she was freezing. When she was a kid, it had been a thrill to walk on fresh snow, to know she was the first to touch it. Now the endless expanse of unblemished snow was simply frightening, like being on a deserted island surrounded by miles of uncrossable ocean.

When Bridget turned away from the window, Bob's eyes were open. He looked exhausted, with hollows in his cheeks and purple shadows under his red, rheumy eyes.

"How're you doing?" she asked softly.

"Not so great." He looked down, and she followed his gaze. The snow in the garbage bags had melted, so now the knotted bags slumped. The skin visible above the makeshift splint was red and swollen.

"I'm so sorry, Bob." She blinked back tears. "I should have thought it through more." Now he might die, and for what? Clearly, no one was coming to save them.

"It's okay." He squeezed his eyes closed and exhaled through clenched teeth.

"Should I take off your scarf? Is it making it hard for you to breathe?"

"No, it's fine. It helps me." He opened his eyes. "A girl gave it to me. Lilly."

"You mentioned her once." Exhaustion made her blunter than she might otherwise have been. "She left you."

His fingers rose to gently touch it. "She didn't leave me. Or at least not the way you think. She died. She had Hodgkin's. Everyone said if you had to have cancer, that was one of the good ones. It still killed her. After she died, I put all my emotions on paper. They couldn't hurt me there." His swallow was loud in the quiet room. "I guess I'll be seeing her soon."

Panic fluttered in Bridget's throat. She was not going to just sit and watch Bob die. "I'm going to beg them to take you to a doctor. Or at least dump you in front of an emergency room and take off."

"Do you honestly think they would do that?"

"What *are* they going to do?"

"I don't know." He sighed. "The thing is, I don't think Derrick and Joanne know either. I just know it can't be anything good." He pasted on a smile. "I would love some morphine, but if I can't have that, I need something to take my mind off the pain. Could you do something for me?"

"Of course. Anything." She nodded vigorously. "What?"

"Read *Eyes of the Forest* to me."

"Didn't Derrick take it?" Last night, he'd picked up the pages next to the typewriter.

He gave her the ghost of a smile. "Do you know the story of Scheherazade?"

"Like in *A Thousand and One Nights*?"

Bob nodded. "The chapters I've been giving Derrick are just shadows of the real book. Good enough to keep him interested, but I saved a better version for myself. And his version isn't finished. Like Scheherazade, my plan was to never finish it, because of what they'd do once it was." He pressed his lips together. Was he thinking of how Bridget had forced their hand? "But at night when Derrick was sleeping, I wrote the real *Eyes of the Forest* and hid the chapters under the treadmill. I finished it the day before you came."

Even here, even now, the idea of reading it thrilled her. "It would be an honor to read it to you."

"Just keep your voice low and be ready to hide it if

one of them comes in. In fact, do it in chunks in case they do come in and catch you. That way I might not lose the whole thing. But I want you to tell me if it's any good."

After retrieving the first stack of about thirty pages, Bridget sat on the floor next to the head of the bed, ready to shove the pages under the nightstand if the door opened. Reading in a low murmur, she found voices for the different characters. Soon she was completely immersed in the story. She no longer thought about what was going to happen to them or Bob's ankle, how hard the floor was, or even possible entries for the database.

Joanne came in only once, carrying four granola bars, two bottles of water, six Tylenol and, oddly, a flower vase. She set everything down on the nightstand. Her expression was grim as she regarded Bob's injury.

Finally she pointed at the vase and addressed Bob. "You can pee in there while I take her to the bathroom." She took the stun gun out of her pocket. "Let's go."

Bridget walked ahead of her, the chain between the shackles rattling with each step. As soon as the door was closed, she inventoried the bathroom. Towels, toothpaste, three toothbrushes, shampoo, a bar of soap. Nothing that could be used as a weapon.

After Joanne brought her back, Bridget read to Bob for another hour. When he fell into an uneasy sleep, Bridget noted the page she was on and kept reading silently to herself. She'd always been a fast reader, and with nothing to distract her, the pages flew by. They were filled with twists and revelations and sudden yet fitting deaths. And woven together with the previous six books, this new one completed a stunning tapestry.

Bridget was only vaguely aware of the real world. The snow finally stopped. At one point she heard Joanne and Derrick talking at the other end of the house. Their voices rose and fell, full of urgency, sometimes overlapping, sometimes rising to a shout. Later she heard shoveling and scraping outside. Then a door slammed, and a motor started up. A car. She barely spared a thought as to whether it was Derrick or Joanne. Did it really matter?

Meanwhile, all too soon, Bridget was on the final page. Her eyes filled with tears as she read the last line.

And he climbed on Grayhorn's back, put his arms around Jancy's waist, and together they flew toward the stars.

After a long moment, Bridget reluctantly put the page down and slid the final stack back under the treadmill. When she turned around, wiping her nose on her sleeve, Bob was awake.

"So you finished it?" he rasped.

"Oh my God, Bob. That—that is an ending."

"Does it work, do you think?" He was watching her closely.

Bridget would have lied if she needed to, but she didn't. "It's"—she sighed—"it's perfect."

She was about to say more when the door handle turned.

Joanne came in, holding the stun gun. "Okay, Bridget, it's time for another bathroom break. And if you promise not to run, I can take off the shackles."

Her heart leapt. "I promise," she lied.

When Joanne bent over to unlock them, Bridget imagined kicking her in the face. Twisting and circling her legs to wrap the chain around the older woman's throat, and then pulling until she passed out and Bridget could retrieve the key and the stun gun from her slack fingers.

Instead, she did nothing, hating herself for her cowardice.

Joanne gestured with the stun gun for Bridget to go into the bathroom. "Stay put until I let you out."

After Bridget flushed the toilet, she waited for Joanne to come back. And waited.

"I'm done," she finally shouted, watching the doorknob, waiting for it to turn. Did she hear footsteps out in the hall? Then the knob rattled. Bridget sucked in a breath, ready to beg for Bob's life as soon as it opened.

But it didn't turn.

And then the footsteps moved away.

Why had Joanne insisted she wait? Bridget's scalp prickled as she reached out her hand and tentatively touched the handle. It turned. But when she tried to push the door open, it only moved an inch before stopping.

She put her eye to the gap. A piece of twine crossed it. One end seemed to be tied to the bathroom doorknob and the other to a doorknob further down the hall.

But why? Why did Joanne need her trapped in the bathroom?"

"Hey," Bridget shouted. "Hey!"

Holding her breath, she strained her ears, but no one

answered. All she heard was an oddly breezy noise. It sounded like a long exhalation. Or a fan? Then outside, she heard a car door slam. A motor started up. It must be Joanne's black Honda. And now it sounded like it was slowly moving away.

But the sound inside the house, the sound she'd heard earlier, was getting louder. Crackling. Whooshing. Bridget sniffed. Smoke.

The house was on fire.

It all made sense now. Seeing Bob grievously injured, Joanne had known that it was time to cut and run. She meant for them to die here. Bridget trapped in the bathroom, Bob immobile in the bedroom. Joanne must have unshackled her in case the stainless steel links survived the fire. She was planning on telling a story with the clues the flames would leave behind. A story about two people caught in an accidental house fire. But shackles on a corpse would be hard to explain away.

The fire would burn this cabin to the ground. And after the authorities found the remains of Bob and his researcher, Joanne would explain, with tears in her eyes, how she'd lent them her family cabin so Bob could finish his book. How an errant candle, lit after the power went out, must have burned everything down.

And then the black market for Bob's last book would go through the roof.

BRIDGET

Too Late

Bridget slammed the bathroom door with her unbruised shoulder until it was as bruised as the other. Kicked it. Ran at it. Each attempt made her gasp with pain, but all it did was stretch the twine a couple of inches. When she tried to squeeze herself through the gap, the space wasn't nearly big enough.

If only she had the Leatherman tool. Which was a stupid thought. Why not wish for a real pair of scissors—or to not be here in the first place?

Then Bridget realized she did have a tool: her teeth. Squishing her face into the gap, she pressed forward until the door's sharp edge on one side and the slightly rounded edge of the frame on the other felt like they might crack her cheekbones.

Finally the twine rested between her lips. Rapidly opening and closing her incisors, she gnashed her teeth. For every time she caught it, there was another when she missed it altogether, her teeth clacking on nothing. She ignored the terrible taste, ignored the smoke getting heavier. Slowly the fibers began to part, covering her tongue in dry, itchy bits.

Finally, the last strand popped and the door flew open. Bridget tumbled forward.

She pushed herself upright. At the end of the hall, fire was beginning to engulf the living room. As she stared, mesmerized, a corner of the upholstered couch went up in yellow flames. Then the fire leapt onto the shade of the lamp next to the couch. The braided rug was smoking. Even if she could somehow get Bob on his feet, by the time they got to the hall, the path to the door would be completely blocked.

That left the window in his room. Now that blanket of snow around the house seemed like a good thing. If she could just get Bob out, at least the fire couldn't follow them.

Which was still a pretty big if.

When she threw open the door to his room, Bob looked at her with wide eyes.

"What's happening?"

She closed the door behind her. "I think Derrick left and then Joanne lit the house on fire and took off."

As she spoke, she tried to raise the window, but it was painted shut. Glad for the protection of her coat, she wrapped her hand in the blanket she'd slept in. She punched the window, but her first blow was too tentative. She had to repeat the move several times, each time with more force and a bigger wince, before it finally broke with a crack. Cold air rushed in as she knocked out the rest of the glass.

"You're bleeding," Bob said.

BOB

Save Yourself

B lood was streaming from a two-inch-long cut on the pinky side of Bridget's right hand. It was clear to Bob that it was not going to stop on its own.

She pressed it against her coat, but that wouldn't work for long. And then Bob's fingers went to the scarf around his throat, as they had so many times before. But this time he wasn't hiding in the comfort of memories.

He unwound it and held it out to her. "Wrap this tight around it. It will stop the bleeding."

Shaking her head, she took a step back. "That's your special scarf. The one that Lilly gave you."

"And if she were here, she would tell you to use it." The crackle of the flames was getting louder. "Hurry."

Bob ended up being the one to quickly wrap it, as Bridget could only use one hand. He finished with a square knot directly on top of the cut. He hated making her wince, but the pressure would encourage it to start closing on its own.

When he finished, she looked at his ankle and then his face. "Do you think you could put any weight on your foot? Just for a second?"

He shook his head. "Even if I wanted to, it wouldn't hold me up." Then he said what needed to be said. "Look, Bridget. You need to get out now before it's too late."

"I can't leave you." Her voice broke.

"But you can't save me. I can't walk. I don't think I could even crawl. It doesn't make any sense for us both to die when you don't have to. Listen to me." His heart cracked open. "Save yourself. I order you to leave me."

"I won't." She raised her chin. "Would Rowan leave Car Umass? Would Margarit leave Jancy?"

"Bridget," he said gently, "they're imaginary. And you're real. You're alive. You have your whole life ahead of you."

"And you've made my life worth living. Just like you did for my mom."

He gripped her uninjured hand. It was warm and dry, a sharp contrast to his own cold, clammy hand. "And if your mom could come back, she would kill me for getting you mixed up in this. You can't save me, child. Save yourself. And if you can, take the book. I'm not worth saving. But that book is. It's the best thing I've ever written."

BRIDGET

Until They Were Dead

Two could play at being stubborn. Bridget set her jaw.
"I won't leave you. So you'd better help me get you
out of here. Sit up."

Bob didn't move. "I can't walk, Bridget."

"All we need to do is get you outside. Then I can drag
you on the quilt." She imagined how that would work.
How quickly the quilt would soak through. How the snow
would start to stick to the fabric, making it heavier and
harder to move.

"I'll be right back," she said. "While I'm gone, sit
yourself up."

With Bob still protesting, she peeked out into the
hall. The smoke was thick as fur, but the flames hadn't
reached the hall quite yet. After closing the bedroom
door, she scurried deeper into the cabin, doubled over and
coughing. She trailed her fingers along the wall until she
reached the bathroom. Gathering the shower curtain into
her arms, she bent her knees to put all her weight on it.

Pop! Pop! Pop! It tore from the rings.

A second later she was running blindly back to Bob.
When she opened the door, the fresh air made the flames

leap forward with a roar. She slammed the door closed, knowing they only had a few minutes. Picking up the garbage bags, now filled with water instead of snow, she put them in front of the door. That might buy them a minute or two.

Bob's face was pale and damp with sweat, but he'd managed to sit up, his legs sticking off the side of the bed. His eyes were closed, his face drawn with pain.

Leaning out the window, Bridget shook out the shower curtain until it was as flat as she could make it. She padded the sill with the blanket. Then she stood on Bob's bad side. "Put your arm around me and your other hand on the table, and stand up. It's, like, three hops, maximum, to the window. Then you'll just sit on the sill and let yourself drop back into the snow."

No time to worry about how neither of them were dressed for freezing weather. How they didn't have shoes. Tendrils of smoke were curling past the door's outlines.

His eyes opened, caught the light. They were watery, but suddenly his focus sharpened. "What about the book?"

"You can always write another book. But there's only one you. Now, on my count of three." She bent her knees. "One." His arm clamped around her shoulder. "Two." His fingers tightened. "Three." She groaned and he moaned as she straightened up and he put his weight on his left leg.

He was standing.

"Okay. Just a couple of hops. One!" His weight almost dragged her off balance as he barely moved an inch.

"Two!" He moved his hand further up the nightstand and then hopped just another few inches. "Three!" Three hops hadn't even cleared the nightstand. "Okay, just a few more and then you can sit on the windowsill."

Bob's breathing sounded like a train trying to build up a head of steam. But finally they reached the window. Bridget tightened her arm around his waist as he took his hand from the nightstand and reached for the sill. But as he did, his bad foot touched the floor. He stiffened like he'd touched a live wire. With a shriek, he tumbled outside.

Her stomach convulsed. Bob lay sprawled on his side, looking lifeless, only half on the shower curtain. It was a relief when he twitched. By now, flames were licking on all sides of the door behind her.

Careful not to step on him, she climbed out after Bob, her stockinged feet punching holes into the snow. As gently as she could, she rolled him on his side and then straightened the shower curtain under him. After rolling him back, she grabbed the curtain on either side of his head. With a grunt, she walked backward, slowly dragging him away from the house and toward the road.

Here was her dad's car, covered with a foot of snow. But the keys were back in the burning house or in Joanne's or Derrick's pocket.

Hunched over, she dragged Bob past it. Her back was starting to spasm, her fingers to cramp. The snow was as deep as her knees, and her feet were already numb, which was almost a blessing.

The house was nearly engulfed in flames, but the snow should stop it from spreading.

Finally, she reached the road, marked by the tracks of Derrick's and Joanne's cars. Her legs were trembling with effort.

If she kept up a steady pace, her feet punching holes through the snow, it wasn't impossible to slide Bob. Every time she paused, though, she lost momentum. To get started again, she had to lean so far back that she nearly fell over. And her steps were short, each one nearly overlapping the one before.

They had only made it about a hundred yards from the house, and she was exhausted. The sweat on her clothes was turning into ice. They weren't going to make three miles. They would be lucky to make another three hundred feet. How long until their fingers and toes were frostbitten? How long until they were hypothermic?

How long until they were dead?

She leaned down and touched Bob's forehead. His eyes opened, but didn't seem to focus. He was nearly as white as the snow, except for bright red cheeks.

After letting out a sob of frustration, Bridget gritted her teeth, grabbed the curtain's crinkling edge, and forced herself to keep moving. What choice did she have?

When she'd driven out here the night before last, this stretch had been nothing but darkness. Not another dwelling for miles. The chance that anyone would notice the fire was minuscule.

And then she heard something far off in the distance behind her. Was—was it a motor? She turned.

A blue snowmobile was racing toward her, going so fast it sometimes caught air.

And in the distance behind it was a white SUV, chains around its tires biting into the snow as it bounced and slewed over drifts.

The snowmobile and then the SUV stopped just short of them. As the snowmobiler turned off his machine, people leapt out of the vehicle.

Bridget must be hallucinating. An old man in clanking armor, a sword at his waist. A girl dressed like an elf and holding a mace. A man wearing wings and knee-high boots, hoisting a shovel like a baseball bat. All three turning their heads back and forth, like they were ready for a fight.

And then the snowmobiler pulled off his helmet and Bridget knew this must be all a dream. Because it was Ajay.

He ran to her, already pulling off his coat. He put it around her shoulders.

"You came," she whispered as he pulled her close.

"I would have been here earlier, but you sent all that information in an email." He tried to laugh, but it sounded more like a sob. "What person our age actually looks at their emails?"

Meanwhile, the fans—for that's what they were, Bridget realized, fans—were kneeling in the snow next to Bob's still figure.

And far in the distance, she heard a sound. A siren.

But were they all too late?

BRIDGET

Freedom

Yes, the person in the pink wings?" Bridget pointed toward the back of the full auditorium. "What's your question?" Forty-five minutes ago, when she and Bob had first walked on stage, she'd expected to feel nervous with hundreds of people staring at her. Instead, the experience had turned out to be oddly serene.

"My question is for both of you. Was it hard to write *Eyes of the Forest* together?"

She and Bob looked at each other. Portland was the first stop on the nineteen-city tour for the new book, which bore both their bylines. *Eyes of the Forest* had only been out for a few days, but it had landed on top of every bestseller list, lauded as the must-read for summer. Even the audiobook, which Bob had insisted Bridget narrate, was smashing sales records.

But the book that had garnered eight starred reviews wasn't the *Eyes of the Forest* Derrick had tried to sell on the dark web. It wasn't even the book Bridget had read in the cabin, the one that had made her weep. The book Bob had urged her to save instead of him. The one that had burned up with the cabin.

It was even better.

Bob took the first crack at answering the question. "Obviously, for me, this was a new way of working. But it turned out to be exactly what was needed to finish the series. Normally in a coauthor situation, you'll see one of two things." He held up a finger. "First, a single writer—usually the less famous of the two—does most or all of the writing, while the more famous one takes most of the credit." He added a second finger. "Or two coauthors will take turns writing from the point of view of a single character." He turned his hand to cut it through the air. "But we didn't do either of those." He looked over at Bridget.

She pulled her mic closer. "First we brainstormed an outline of the book. That was new for Bob, but he says it really helped." Next to her, Bob nodded. "Then we each picked which chapters we wanted to write. Bob called it putting the meat on the bones, and that part went really fast. Once one of us had finished a chapter, we emailed it to the other, who then used track changes to suggest edits. It was a little complicated, but it worked for us."

Bob pointed at another waving hand. "The person dressed as, if I'm not mistaken, Prince Orwen?"

The questioner, who looked to be in his late teens, grinned at being recognized. "How much did it hurt to have the books burn up in that cabin?"

The audience murmured as the Powell's events coordinator jumped to her feet. "I made it clear that they would not be taking any questions about what happened."

"I'll answer this one, but after that, no more, okay?" Bob said.

The police had asked Bridget and Bob not to speak publicly about the kidnapping. If they had been hoping to keep a lid on information, it hadn't worked. The bizarre chain of events had been covered extensively in newspapers, magazines, and blogs, and on TV, radio, Twitter, Facebook, Instagram, podcasts, and even TikTok. All six previous Swords and Shadows books returned to the bestseller lists. Five weeks after the fire, an unauthorized book about their kidnappings had been rushed out, filled with blurry screenshots from the Haldon Cam. And of course Reddit was overrun with threads about every conceivable aspect of the case.

When Bridget had climbed on the treadmill desk to broadcast their plea, most people had thought it was just part of some elaborate joke or hoax. But a handful had called the police. Derrick had as well, with a slightly different and equally fantastic story. The police had eventually decided to dispatch a couple of officers to check things out.

At the same time, a group of rabid fans who lived nearby and had an SUV with chains and four-wheel drive had decided to drive out and see for themselves. Believing it might be a secret fan cosplay event, they had dressed for the part.

As for Ajay, he had borrowed his neighbor's snowmobile and loaded it into his dad's pickup, switching to it when the snow got too heavy. After at first dismissing Bridget's emails, he had seen a screen capture of her desperate plea on Reddit and realized she was telling the truth.

Now Bob said, "At the time, I honestly thought Bridget should prioritize saving the manuscript. I didn't think I was going to make it. But thankfully, she had more faith than I did." They exchanged a grin.

Bridget saw a healthy Bob, one who finally no longer needed a cane. In her mind's eye, though, she saw the cops trying to load a nearly comatose Bob into the back of their SUV, desperate to get him to the hospital.

The physical therapists had credited Bob's recovery after surgery to set the bone to the fact that he was in pretty good shape from Joanne and Derrick's enforced diet and exercise routine. After he was discharged, he'd even bought a treadmill desk for his home office.

Bridget had given police the tracker information for Joanne's car. After being pulled over on her way to the airport, she had been arrested. Her trial was still months off. Derrick had accepted a plea deal that avoided jail time in return for his cooperation. He was now attending an alternative high school, in court-ordered therapy, and living with his dad. He was still allowed to LARP.

Bridget chose the next questioner, a wide-eyed girl of about twelve. Even though the girl had dark hair, there was something about her that reminded Bridget of herself at that age.

"My question is for Mr. Haldon. Where's your scarf?"

Bridget caught her breath.

Bob put his fingertips to his bare neck. "I used to think I needed to wear the scarf to remind me of the person who it originally belonged to. But then I realized she's always with me." His smile was tinged with sadness.

"And there's a freedom in not always wearing the same thing. Not always writing the same thing."

He smiled and pointed at a woman in her fifties dressed in a sundress.

"What's next for you two?"

Bridget answered first. "Well, I still have a year of high school. And I'm thinking about where I might want to go to college. Meanwhile, a friend is teaching me to cook this summer." Her eyes went to Ajay, who was sitting in a reserved seat in the front row right next to her dad. Now he grinned and gave her a thumbs-up. He was still a little bit in awe of how big a deal Bob really was.

The woman in the sundress rephrased her question. "What about writing? Are you two working on anything new?"

Bridget and Bob exchanged a look. "There might be a little something in the works," he said. They had started brainstorming a prequel set in the same universe as Swords and Shadows, but featuring a seventeen-year-old girl. A girl who had no magic. A girl a lot like the one Bridget had started writing about earlier.

At that, the woman started to clap, and soon the whole audience had joined in. Bob nodded at Bridget. Together, they got to their feet and took a bow.

LARPing. While LARPing, people take on the personas and abilities of someone other than themselves and then act out adventures.

Folks at the Barony of Three Mountains, my local chapter of the Society for Creative Anachronism (SCA) let me observe their combat event, which featured armored participants. SCA is a medieval living history organization re-creating the arts and skills of pre-seventeenth-century Europe.

Macmillan Publishing's anti-piracy manager, Catherine Bogin, helped me think about the ins and outs of selling illegally obtained book chapters on the dark web.

My agent, Wendy Schmalz, was a rock as we both learned to navigate the new pandemic world.

My editor, Christy Ottaviano, helped me figure out how to make this book the best it could be.

Associate editor Jessica Anderson has a sharp eye and keeps us all organized. Publicist Morgan Rath, who normally helps me with planes, trains, and automobiles, pivoted to help me with Zoom. Mike Burroughs designed the eye-catching cover, and Lelia Mander handled the copyediting and proofreading, with the help of Ana Deboo and Bonnie Cutler. Other wonderful folks at Macmillan include Lucy Del Priore, Katie Halata, Melissa Croce, Molly Brouillette Ellis, and Kathryn Little.

A NOTE FROM THE AUTHOR

I think every writer, if they write long enough, eventually writes a book where one of the main characters is a writer. *Eyes of the Forest* is mine.

Bridget was named in honor of Bridget Zinn, an amazing young adult author who died from colon cancer at 33. Check out her lovely book, *Poison*. So many people helped me pull this book together. Any errors are my own.

Joe Collins, a firefighter and paramedic, helped me figure out if handcuffs would melt in a fire as well as how to treat a compound fracture. Paul Dreyer, CEO of Avid4 Adventure (avid4.com), who was my wilderness medicine instructor when I was researching *Playing with Fire*, answered questions about fractures and infections.

Robin Burcell, a former cop and now bestselling author, helped me understand how my fictional cops would view fans.

Don Read at Pacific Typewriter did not even blink when I showed up at his shop with a pair of handcuffs and questions about whether it would be possible to snap off a typewriter part and use it to shim your way out of handcuffs. (The answer is yes, if you use the part called the ribbon vibrator.)

Krystina Foelker, who is active in Refuge LARP, a local Live Action Role Play, helped me understand